"We have all known the long loneliness and we have
learned that the only solution is love and that
love comes with community."

—Dorothy Day

Love's a Mystery

Love's a Mystery

in

Deadwood
OR

Emily Quinn &
Laura Bradford

Guideposts

Published by Guideposts
100 Reserve Road, Suite E200
Danbury, CT 06810
Guideposts.org

Cover and interior design by Müllerhaus
Cover illustration by Dan Burr at Illustration Online LLC.
Typeset by Aptara, Inc.

ISBN 978-1-961441-42-2 (hardcover)
ISBN 978-1-961441-43-9 (softcover)
ISBN 978-1-959633-14-3 (epub)

Printed and bound in the United States of America

LOVE IS
AN ART

by
EMILY QUINN

*Therefore each of you must put off falsehood
and speak truthfully to your neighbor, for we are
all members of one body.*

—Ephesians 4:25 (niv)

CHAPTER ONE

On the road to Portland, Oregon
1950

Roberta Stevens wiggled in the hard bus seat, trying to get comfortable. She'd spent the last six hours staring out the window, wondering how she could have been so wrong. Not only was she not Mrs. Philip Collins today, but the man she'd given her heart to had left town with the money they'd been gifted by friends and family to start their new life together. All she had left was thirty dollars and this bus ticket to Portland, Oregon. Thank goodness Mama always preached that Roberta should keep some pin money on her. When she'd bought the ticket in St. Louis, the ticket agent had looked at her like she was insane. Now, watching the miles go past, one field at a time, she was starting to agree with his assessment. She still had her pride, but what did that do for her in this situation?

Roberta pulled up the edges of her now not-so-white gloves as she considered her situation. One thing she knew for certain. She couldn't have stayed in St. Louis. Every time her friends looked at her, she'd know what they were thinking. *Poor Roberta, she was clueless.* She touched the neckline of her shirt and felt Grandma's pearls around her neck. Those pearls and the engagement ring that she still wore were her reserves. The ring she would sell as soon as she arrived in Portland, provided it was worth anything. Since Philip had tried to get her to give it to him the night before their wedding, saying he wanted to get it attached to the wedding ring before the ceremony, it probably was worth something. At least enough to get her settled. Even if it was in a rented room while she looked for work.

When he didn't show up at the church on their wedding day, at first she thought he was angry about her refusal to give him the ring. Then her friend's husband went to the boardinghouse, and Philip's room was empty. Instead of standing at the altar waiting for her, he was gone. Along with all his belongings and the gifts that people had given them before the wedding. When she realized he wasn't going to show, she thanked everyone for coming and asked them to take the presents they'd brought back home with them. There would be no need for a new set of linens or even the quilt her grandmother had made for Roberta's wedding bed. She had no groom.

Roberta blinked away tears as she smoothed a wrinkle out of her skirt. The saleswoman had assured her that the fabric was perfect for traveling and wouldn't wrinkle during the long drive to their Florida honeymoon and a new life. She'd been wrong. Everything was wrong. Moving and starting over had been Philip's idea. Philip's plan. He was probably already in Florida. Sitting on the beach he'd promised her, with a cold drink in his hand.

Now, thinking of a drink made her thirsty. But the mason jar she'd brought from her apartment and refilled with water at the last stop was already empty. The bus driver talked about making good time and limiting the stops they made, so she didn't know when she'd be able to refill it.

A bottle of orange soda came into view from her left. She turned and saw that the seat next to her had been taken by a large man in a black suit. He wore a fedora and carried a tan case, much like her own that she had slid under the seat. "Excuse me, miss," he said, holding out the bottle, "but you look thirsty. It's awfully dry and hot on this bus."

She forced a smile. Just because she was out of sorts didn't mean she should be rude. "I don't want to take your soda."

"You're not taking if I give it to you freely." He smiled kindly at her. "Besides, I'm only doing my Christian duty. I can't let a fellow traveler thirst next to me when I bought two sodas at our last stop."

Roberta reached to take it, but then she paused. "I'm afraid I don't know your name."

He took his hat off, and Roberta noticed the thin comb-over of brown hair on the top of his head. He reminded her of her father. He took a handkerchief out of his suit pocket and wiped the sweat from his brow. "Robert Smith. But please, call me Bob."

"Well, we have something in common. Were you named after your father?" Roberta stared at the man sitting next to her as she accepted the opened soda. She took a sip, and the sugary orange taste brightened her mood. What was it about a treat that made one instantly feel better about the world? "Thank you for the soda. You were right, it's just what I needed."

"I *was* named after my father. How did you know? He would have been very proud, since now his name is part of the United States Postal Service. I have my commission papers right here." He dug into his case and showed her a letter of introduction from the United States Postal Service. He pointed to the name on the letter.

"See? Robert Nelson Smith. The new postmaster of Deadwood, Oregon. Although, I'm not so certain I'm the man for the job."

"Congratulations on the posting. I'm sure you'll be great. I was also named after my father. I'm Roberta Stevens." She took another small sip. The man—*Bob*—she corrected herself, not only was around her father's age, but he ran a post office. Mama would have said he was bona fide with those credentials and safe to talk with. But, then again, her mother had loved Philip from the start as well. Maybe no one in Roberta's family had good taste in men. "I appreciate the soda. I'll buy you one at the next stop."

"No need. I'm just hoping the stop will be long enough for me to take a short walk around the bus station. My legs are beginning to cramp." He glanced out the window. "I was hoping to be able to stay in St. Louis. I was courting someone, but when she heard where I was going, she wasn't interested in living in such a small town."

"I'm sorry. Did you love her?" Roberta held up her hand. "Sorry again to be so personal. I'm not sure what's gotten into me."

"It's riding the bus." He smiled, which made her relax. "You feel like you can tell your seatmate anything, since you'll probably never see them again. I'll go first. I was in love with Harriet, and leaving her behind has made me question even taking this job. I'm pretty sure the only reason I'm doing so is to please my parents. There, that feels better to say it out loud. Thank you for listening. What about you? What secret are you holding that you need to tell someone?"

She took a deep breath and then blurted it out. All of it. How Philip had wooed her then betrayed her and stolen their wedding money. "Now I feel like a fool. So I'm starting over. New life, new opportunities, in Portland."

"That's quite a story. You're a brave woman, Roberta Stevens. I'm proud to have met you." He yawned and tucked his case under the bench seat in front of them. "This heat is making me sleepy. Wake me when we get to the next stop, okay, Roberta?"

"Of course." Roberta went back to staring out the window. So much for having someone to talk to. It had been nice to tell someone everything. Someone who wouldn't call her naive or judge her for making poor decisions. It must be a sign that she was doing the right thing. She finished the soda, and the sound of the tires beating the road, combined with the warm summer sun coming in the window, lulled her into sleep as well.

When she woke, she was alone on the bus. She checked her earrings to see if they'd fallen off while she slept. They were still there. As were the ring and the pearls, and she saw her case under the seat. The driver had stopped the bus at a way station. She ran into him as she went down the aisle and exited the bus.

"You only have ten minutes, so I suggest you speed up if you don't want to be left behind in Nebraska." He was eating a sandwich, and Roberta's stomach growled at the smell. He grinned. "Food's at the far end of the station by the restrooms. I'll wait for you, but hurry."

She rushed toward the station door. She needed to find the ladies' room, fill her water jar, and buy the cheapest sandwich she could find plus a soda for Mr. Smith.

Eleven minutes later, her list complete, she climbed back onto the bus. "I made it!" Out of breath, she grinned at the driver.

"You're lucky I'm a good guy." He glanced at his watch then looked up at her and matched her grin. "I'm just teasing you. We're still missing a passenger. I couldn't have left anyway. Go find your seat, and I'll see what's keeping the other guy."

She moved though row after row of shoulders, trying not to step on anyone's foot. No one even looked up as she passed by. She'd been right in her first decision as an unengaged woman. Escaping St. Louis was the best way to forget about Philip and the life he'd promised she'd be living right now.

Her row was empty. Bob Smith must be the missing passenger.

She slid into the window seat and looked around to see if Mr. Smith had changed seats. No, he wasn't on the bus. She watched out the window as a police officer came up to the driver outside the station. They talked for a few minutes, and then the driver got back on the bus.

"We're on our way to Portland. Settle in and get some sleep while I take care of the driving," he announced over the intercom.

Roberta hurried up front. "The man who was sitting next to me isn't on the bus," she said to the driver.

"Did you know him?"

Roberta shook her head. "No. We talked for a few minutes, but I didn't know him."

The driver nodded at the station, where the police officer had disappeared inside. "I'm sorry, but no one can find him. We can't wait forever. The officer has his information, so we'll get him on the next bus when he shows up."

"Oh my goodness." Roberta nervously looked around the now empty parking lot. "He said he wanted to stretch his legs."

"He knew how long we were going to be here. I told everyone who got off the bus. Miss, you need to get in your seat. We've got to get this bus going so we're not late pulling into our next stop." He started the engine and turned away from her.

Roberta retreated down the aisle. Now people were watching her, wondering why she was delaying their trip. She sank into her seat and studied the gathering night. She couldn't see anyone near the building. Maybe they'd find Mr. Smith walking down the road. It really wasn't her concern, but she had wanted to repay him for the soda.

After she finished eating and they'd gone miles past the way station, she decided to pull out her drawing pad and focus on the sunset they were driving into rather than the nice man who'd missed the bus. She picked up her case and pulled out a leather folder. *What in the world?* She didn't have a leather folder. She opened the case wider and realized her pad was gone. As were her drawing pencils.

She glanced around the seats, but most people were asleep. Who would steal papers and pencils anyway? She opened the leather folder and realized it was the commission paperwork for the Deadwood Post Office. She had Bob Smith's case. The gold engraving on the outside said *RS*. Just like hers did. She bent down to look under the seats and used her foot to check for another case. Nothing.

Her case was gone. All of her art supplies—her colored pencils, her notebook, her brushes—gone. And she had Mr. Smith's case instead. She put the commission back into the folder and put the case under the seat. Nothing was going her way today.

Tears began to blur her eyes. She tried to will them away. She could buy more art supplies when she got settled. Crying over Philip's betrayal would be fruitless. She let her emotions settle, and then she checked the map they'd given her when she bought the ticket. They would stop in Deadwood on their way to Portland.

She'd just get off, leave the case and the commission with the sheriff, then be on her way. It was the right thing to do.

She wiped the tears from her face and took off her jacket to use as a blanket. Tomorrow would be better. It had to be.

Jonathan Devons nodded to his foreman, Roland Farmer, as he left the lumber mill for the night. *A good day's work*, Roland had called out to the crew as they finished cutting the last log into boards. Jonathan knew it was a dangerous day's work as well, but after the money he'd brought with him had run out, he needed a job. Deadwood wasn't a busy metropolis like Chicago, where he'd come from. He'd been lucky to find a job at all. Roland was kin to the woman who ran the boardinghouse where he'd gotten a room, and she'd taken a shine to him, as his mother would say. Jonathan thought the shine was more for her daughter, who didn't look old enough to be out of school, much less looking for a husband.

But things worked differently here. Or maybe they worked like this everywhere and Jonathan had never noticed. He'd been betrothed to one woman since his college graduation. Now that was over, and he was apparently back on the market, whether he wanted to be or not. He took his cap off and brushed the sawdust out of his hair. He'd need to get it cut sooner rather than later, as he was looking a little ragged. Even for someone who worked with his hands and not at the corporate offices he'd left behind in Chicago.

He dodged a car that had turned onto the only paved street in town. Deadwood was on the highway that went north to Portland

and south to Eugene. He hadn't decided which way he'd go when he left, but he wanted to get to the coast and see the ocean before he settled down anywhere. Seeing the car reminded him of his own sedan, sitting outside the boardinghouse like a yard ornament. There wasn't much of a reason to drive the few blocks to the lumber mill every morning. He saw his car as his own magic carpet, like in the Aladdin stories. Just waiting to take him to his next adventure.

Instead of heading directly to the boardinghouse and his room to wash up and wait for dinner, he turned toward the town square, which was a park with a fountain in the middle and a few benches scattered around it. The city offices and the general store surrounded the park as did the just-completed post office and another building that soon would be a new library if the town got a Carnegie grant. The building that currently held the small book collection was off the park, not grand enough for the current town fathers to provide funding or a proper building.

Or at least that was his take on the discussions occurring at work and at the dinner table. He tried to stay out of Deadwood politics, but Mrs. Elliott liked her guests to be current on the local gossip. Especially when they were here for more than a week, like Jonathan had been. He'd had enough of politics at his father's dinner table to last a lifetime. Maybe parents and children always came down on the opposite side of the events of the day. At least he had. His brother hadn't cared one way or another.

Jonathan leaned back on the white park bench, watching the town around him. He always said that writers were like magpies—they picked up little bits and pieces everywhere and used them in their books. His book. He rubbed his face. He hadn't worked on his novel for days. Okay, maybe it had been weeks. He'd left the typewriter at home. It was too bulky to pack with him on what the Australians would call a walkabout. His journal would have to do. However, all he'd been writing in the journal lately was his days' activities.

The last few entries had looked the same. Seven a.m. wake up. Coffee and breakfast at the boardinghouse. Then to work, where he took trees cut down in the forest and made them into boards. Boards for new houses and barns. Boards for new stores and the new post office. Deadwood was booming and needed a lot of boards. After work, he'd come here to the park and sit for a while so the muse could visit. And when it didn't, he'd close his journal and tuck it into his pocket. Then go to dinner at the boardinghouse, while away a couple of hours, and fall asleep while trying to read under the dim light in his room.

And the next day he'd do the same.

Even his muse was bored.

Maybe the idea of a novel was presumptuous. His professors had warned him that the publishing industry was a hard life. They'd tried to steer him toward editing or accounting, where he could work in the book world and still eat, if not earn enough to have a family.

He'd tried to explain this to his father the day he'd graduated, but Father had told him what his future was going to be. He was joining the family construction business and marrying a proper match. Since Jonathan hadn't found a suitable wife during his college years, the family had a solution. No muss, no fuss. Everything was settled.

Except Jonathan hadn't wanted the life his father had set up for him, including the ready-made wife. And now, he was reliving the same day over and over. Paying penance for leaving Chicago? For rejecting the life he'd been given? Or was this just the way life worked?

Either way, Jonathan needed a change. He mentally calculated how much money he had set aside, not counting his trust. He didn't have quite enough to get him to a bigger town, but he was getting close. Maybe next week he'd pack up the sedan and leave. Three weeks at the max. Which would give the parcel he was waiting for time to arrive. Once the new journal came, he'd start working on his book. He was sure of it. There was nothing like a new journal to get the juices flowing.

He closed his eyes and listened to the birds chirping. Now that he had a plan in place, things didn't look so bleak. Or so boring. By fall, he'd be settled in a new job and a new life. And he could forget his old life completely. Reinvention number two?

He watched the bus coming down the street. Maybe the driver would bring mail with him. His mother would say the bus was a sign. But then, she believed in signs. He didn't. He believed in hard work. Signs led you astray.

Jonathan gathered his pen and journal and put them in his jacket pocket. Then he followed the bus to its stopping point next to the general store. *God rewards those who wait*, he thought as he lingered on the porch to see if the driver dropped off a bag of mail.

He was doing the work. Now he just needed to complete the plan. Things were looking up.

CHAPTER TWO

The passengers disembarked as if they were waking up from a long sleep. Except for the children, who bounced off the bus step like they were on pogo sticks. Bursting with energy they'd been holding in during the bus ride, they seemed poised to explode or at least stampede their way to the food stand with their less energetic parents.

Jonathan smiled and patted his jacket pocket. He'd have something to write about tonight after dinner. The comparison between the children and the adults as they got off the bus. There might be a story there. He pondered the thought as one last passenger got off the bus and caught his attention.

The woman was slender, dressed in a travel suit complete with earrings and white gloves. Her red hair was pulled into a bun, but strands were trying to escape the confinement. She blew away a lock that tried to cover her face. In her arms, she had a tan case, and she was holding it close to her chest. Her money was probably in the case. He turned to look at the children again, but his attention wandered back to see what the woman was doing.

She appeared younger than him. Maybe mid-twenties. But determination burned on her face. She glanced around the street, her gaze finding his. He smiled again, knowing just how to match his eyes to the emotion to get a return smile, but this time, it didn't happen. Instead, she headed directly toward him, and he felt his heart rate increase. Surprised by his reaction, he hardly had time to prepare a proper hello, as she was almost on top of him. "Good evening—"

She swept past him.

Startled, he spun around and watched as she stepped up on the sidewalk and entered the general store.

He blinked and thought about dinner, which was probably ready at the boardinghouse. He thought of the pages he wanted to write about the bouncing children and their half-asleep parents. And then he did something that surprised himself. He followed her into the general store.

The young woman who managed the front of the shop smiled at him. What was her name? Amanda? Mandy? No, it was Amanda. She'd been making conversation and dropping hints for the last several days that she was available for an evening stroll after work. "Good evening, Jonathan. Can I assume you came to chat, since you typically come much earlier?"

He shook his head, scanning the room. "Sorry, I didn't." A quick glance her way showed him the disappointment on her face, but he'd been clear that he wasn't interested in a relationship. That was the last thing he needed. Something to tie him to this too-small town and the job at the lumber mill.

He moved toward the back where he spied the woman from the bus talking to Mr. Chase, the store owner. For the last few years, Mr. Chase had also been the unofficial postmaster of Deadwood. He'd told Jonathan he was eager to give up the job as soon as the new postmaster arrived.

The woman handed over the case, and Mr. Chase set it on the counter. Jonathan got closer so he could hear their conversation, pretending to be interested in the week-old newspaper out of Portland that was still for sale.

"Well, that is disappointing news. I'm not sure how much longer I can keep up this job as well as running the store." Mr. Chase ran a hand through his hair. The man might be in his fifties, but he still looked young. Even with juggling two jobs.

"I'm sure Mr. Smith will be arriving any day now to open the post office. He was very excited about the position." Apparently the woman was trying to make Mr. Chase feel better about her news. "I really need to get some supplies before I get back on the bus. We still have a long way to Portland."

Jonathan saw the idea as soon as it hit Mr. Chase. Now this was interesting. He was glad he'd postponed his dinner to see how this played out.

"Now, Miss…" Mr. Chase looked up at her, his eyebrows raised.

"Stevens. Roberta Stevens," she said, apparently not suspecting the offer that Jonathan had already guessed was coming.

"What a lovely name. Do you have family in Portland? A job?"

Miss Stevens dropped her head. She was definitely hiding something that she didn't want to admit to Mr. Chase. Jonathan saw a secret. Mr. Chase? He saw a weakness and an opportunity. "No, I'm starting over. I'm sure I'll find a suitable position when I arrive. I've been working as a clerk in a large St. Louis company for several years now."

"Well then, I have a proposition for you. We are missing our postmaster, and I need to hand off the responsibilities. With your experience, I'm sure you can handle the job. I have a manual I'll give you along with the keys to the new building. You can set the office up for Mr. Smith, and then when he arrives, you can be on your way to Portland. With some money in your pocket for your trouble." Mr. Chase pushed the case back toward her and set a thick book on top of it. "What do you say? Can you help me out? The town will cover your expenses here while we wait."

"I..." Miss Stevens looked stunned. Jonathan could see the wheels turning in her head. "I have nowhere to stay."

He stepped forward. "Mr. Chase, Miss...Stevens, is it? I couldn't help overhearing some of your conversation. I know that my landlady, Mrs. Elliott, has been holding a room for the new postmaster, and it's causing an issue for her, financially. I'm sure she'd let you rent the room until the new postmaster arrives."

"Oh Jonathan, what a good idea." Mr. Chase nodded enthusiastically. "Miss Stevens, it seems like we've solved your problem as well as Mrs. Elliott's."

Miss Stevens turned to Jonathan, and now he could see that her eyes were emerald green. And wary. "I'm on my way to Portland," she repeated.

Mr. Chase laughed. "My dear, Portland will be there next week. From what you've said, this arrangement might only be for a few days, since Mr. Smith is on his way. Another bus will pass through at the end of the week, and I'm sure he'll be on it. You look like you could use a good night's sleep in a real bed and not on that creaky bus. And I really need your help."

Miss Stevens bit her bottom lip.

Jonathan held his breath. He didn't know why he was invested in this woman accepting Mr. Chase's offer, but he was. It must be the writer in him. It was the first thing that had happened in Deadwood since he'd arrived that was interesting enough to write about. He waited for her answer.

As Roberta walked out of the general store and toward the bus, her head was spinning. She'd only wanted to give the case to someone who would return it to Mr. Smith. If he ever showed up. If not, she guessed the commission paperwork would need to be returned to the main office and reissued to a new postmaster. She glanced over at the man walking beside her. Tall, dark hair, and with humor in his blue eyes, he was just her type. Which meant she shouldn't even be thinking about him. She didn't need a man. She'd be one of those old maids who designed her own life and maybe raised cats. She liked animals. Cats would be good company.

Roberta held her hand up to get the driver's attention.

He was eating another sandwich. "Yes, miss? Did you find someone to take the case? We only have ten more minutes here, then we'll be on our way."

"Actually, I've had a change in my travel plans. Can you get my suitcase for me, please? It's plaid, and here's the ticket." She took out the ticket they'd given her to reclaim her suitcase in Portland.

"You're staying here, then?" The driver took the ticket and went to the back of the bus. He opened the door and lifted himself inside. "Oh, it's right here."

Roberta let out a sigh when she saw it really was her suitcase. She'd been worried about handing it over to the man at the station, as he'd just thrown it onto a cart next to him. *Trust others*, she reminded herself. Then she remembered Philip and amended the thought. "I've been offered a job for a few days. The man who missed the bus was expected here."

The driver held out the suitcase, and the man beside her stepped in to take it. The driver met his gaze before releasing the luggage. He jumped off the bus and shut the back door, checking the hold before turning around to talk to Roberta. "Well, I hope it works out for you. If not, I'll be here at the end of the week, and you can continue your journey then."

Roberta blew out a breath. At least she had an escape plan in case things weren't how Mr. Chase had explained. She'd heard rumors of women being abducted in the west, but that had been years ago when the area was wild. Deadwood, despite the name, seemed like a normal town, even it if was a little small. And Mr. Chase had been right about the bed. She craved a good night's sleep.

"The boardinghouse is this way, Miss Stevens." The man who held her suitcase nodded toward the other end of town.

Her hand pressed against her neck. Grandma's pearls were still there, hidden under her suit. She tucked her purse under her arm, checking once more for the outline of the ring on her right hand. Her case was with the missing Mr. Smith. So inside this suitcase was almost everything she owned. Somehow it seemed like not very much to start a new life with. "Thank you. I should buy something to eat first, however."

"Dinner is probably on the table and waiting for us. Mrs. Elliott told me she was planning on chicken and dumplings for tonight's meal." The man smiled. "I have to admit that the food she serves is very good. I hadn't been expecting the meals to be quite so tasty here in Oregon. I guess I believed Chicago had the best food in the country."

She turned and looked at him as they walked. "Oh, so you're not from Deadwood?"

He laughed and shook his head. "I was on a road trip and stopped for a meal. The next thing I knew, I had a job and was staying at Mrs. Elliott's boardinghouse. I'm not planning on staying long."

"So we have something in common." Roberta smiled in spite of her misgivings. "I'm from the St. Louis area, myself. I'm sorry, I didn't catch your name."

"My apologies, where are my manners. I'm Jonathan Devons. Please call me Jonathan. Nice to meet you, Miss Stevens."

"If you're Jonathan, then I'm Roberta." She indicated the large house with the big porch and full front yard. "That house is beautiful. The colors of the flowers with the white clapboard makes it almost glow in the evening light."

"That's our boardinghouse. Tomorrow, before I go to work, I'll walk you over to the new post office. Mr. Chase gave you a key, correct?" He turned up the sidewalk.

Roberta patted her pocket. "Right here. Although I have no idea what I'll be doing. Mr. Chase gave me a manual, so I'll need to read up on the care and feeding of a post office before throwing open the door. I'll just set it up for the real postmaster."

"Something gives me the feeling that you'll have the post office up and running very soon. You seem very determined." He held the door open for her. "Mrs. Elliott? You have a new guest."

Roberta paused in the entryway and admired a painting. It looked familiar, but maybe it was a copy of a well-known artist's work. She'd find an art book and look it up as soon as she got to Portland.

Jonathan pointed to the room to her left, and she followed him inside.

A middle-aged woman was leaning over the table, filling bowls from a large casserole dish. A teenage girl sat on her right, staring at Jonathan like he was one of the dishes being served. Three men sat on the other side of the table, and a woman sat on the end. There were two chairs left. One with a place setting next to the young girl, and one empty. "Oh my, no one told me you were coming," Mrs. Elliott said. "You must have gotten off the bus?"

Roberta found herself being bustled into the dining room. After Jonathan introduced her to the others, he had her sit at the table where the silverware was set.

"Constance, be a dear and get a place setting for Mr. Devons," Mrs. Elliott said to her daughter. "You'll be staying with us for a while, Miss Stevens? I only have one room available, and the new postmaster is supposed to be arriving any day."

"Actually, Roberta's taking on the postmaster job while we wait for his arrival." Jonathan set her bag by the stairs. "The town is covering her costs until Mr. Smith arrives."

"Well, isn't that perfect then." Mrs. Elliott looked relieved as she dished up a bowl of the chicken and dumplings and set it in front of Roberta. "Eat, dear. You look like you haven't had a proper meal in weeks."

"I've had a few things going on," Roberta admitted as her stomach growled. The others were eating and politely ignoring the newcomer, even though she could see interest and questions on their faces. She picked up a spoon and took a bite. The dish was better than her grandmother's chicken and dumplings recipe. She held up a dumpling on her spoon. "I've never seen them done this way. Grandma always made flat, noodle-like dumplings."

"These are egg drop dumplings. So much faster. Some days I do raised dumplings when I have a bit more time, but mostly, that's what you get around here." Mrs. Elliott dished out a bowl for Jonathan. "Here you go. You were late and missed the prayer. I thought maybe that brother of mine was making you work longer. I heard you got an order for the new church down the street."

"Yes, we started on that today." He turned to Roberta and explained. "I work at the lumber mill, making boards."

"And you're a writer," Constance added as she handed him some silverware.

He blushed. "I'm not a writer. Writing is my hobby."

Roberta watched as he focused on his dinner. "I'm a painter. I love drawing landscapes and portraits."

"Oh, that's lovely, dear," Mrs. Elliott said from the end of the table. "Do you dabble, or are you a professional?"

Roberta shook her head. "I went to art school for a couple of years, but I had to drop out to help support my family. Professionally, I'm a clerk, I guess. And tomorrow I'll be a postal worker. Paperwork is all the same. A lot of organizing and keeping track of what goes where. The work isn't especially thrilling, but I enjoy finishing projects."

"As a woman, I'd expect you'd be looking for a husband and starting a family. What are you, twenty-five?" The man across from her pointed his spoon at her. "Time's wasting. You need to find a suitable man and forget all this working and painting nonsense."

"Now, Gerald. Women aren't just jumping into marriage these days. Some want a career and don't mind being single." Mrs. Elliott smiled at Roberta.

Something about the smile wasn't as supportive as her words. Before she could respond, Constance spoke.

"Women are allowed to work outside the home. Remember all the women who worked during the war? We would have lost without women in factories or making deliveries. I'm going to college and then having a job for at least five years before I get married. I want to be able to take care of my family like my mother has after my father died." Constance covered her mom's hand with her own. "I don't want to have to depend on anyone to put food on my table or clothes on my back."

"My child, women aren't strong enough to bring home the bacon, so to speak. The man is the head of the household. He's the one who is supposed to take care of the outside world. Your job is to make a lovely home, like your mother has done here at the boardinghouse." Gerald held out his bowl. "May I get more of this tasty dish? You should be teaching your daughter to cook like you do."

"What about Rosie the Riveter? She was a hero because she stepped in and kept everything going here at home." Constance squared her shoulders.

"Constance." Mrs. Elliott shook her head.

Constance rolled her eyes and picked up her spoon. "Fine. I'm sorry I was so direct."

"My daughter has her own mind on who and what she's going to be when she grows up. We're living in a changing world, Gerald. You need to get used to it." Mrs. Elliott smiled at her daughter as she refilled his bowl. Then she turned to Roberta. "How long do you think you'll be staying in Deadwood, Miss Stevens?"

Roberta didn't say what she wanted to—hopefully not long. Instead she said, "If you keep serving meals like this, my time here won't be long enough."

Jonathan beamed at her. Mrs. Elliott blushed. Only Gerald seemed to not like the answer or the fact that she was sitting at the table with him. A single woman with no current plans to marry.

Well, what he thought of her wasn't her problem. She had enough things to juggle. His opinion wasn't even on the first few pages of her worry list.

✑ CHAPTER THREE ✑

While Roberta waited for Jonathan to meet her in the small foyer area of the boardinghouse the next morning, she wandered around, looking at the pictures and paintings hanging on the floral wallpaper.

"That's my late husband, Wilfred, and me on our wedding day. Getting the picture taken was terribly expensive and not something a young couple should be spending their money on, but Wilfred insisted," Mrs. Elliott said from behind her. She walked over and touched the frame of the small black-and-white photo on the wall. "I'm especially in love with any of the Renaissance-era reproductions. Of course, even those can be pricey."

Roberta pointed to the painting she'd seen last night. "That one is lovely."

"It is, isn't it? I especially like that one."

Jonathan appeared at the top of the stairs. Even just looking at him took Roberta's breath away. She shook off the unsolicited emotion. "I guess I'm off to my new job. It's only temporary, but it still feels like the first day of school."

Mrs. Elliott looked around and lowered her voice. "It doesn't matter what Gerald or men like him say, women do a lot to keep things going these days. The war changed the world. We can do all kinds of jobs, including keeping the post office running when no one else steps up to do it. I'm very happy you decided to stay in Deadwood, even though it may be a short visit."

"Good morning, ladies," Jonathan said when he reached the bottom stair. "You seem to be in the middle of a conversation. I can wait outside for you, Roberta, if you wish."

"We were just talking about how excited Miss Stevens is about starting her new job." Mrs. Elliott smiled at Jonathan. "I hope you two have a good day at work. I'm washing sheets today, since it should be a nice, sunny day for them to dry."

Roberta took one last glance at the painting. It looked like it should be on a museum wall and not in a small boardinghouse in Oregon. She'd love to sit and study it, but she had a job to do. "Are we ready to go? I'd hate to be late on my first day."

"Since you're your own boss until Mr. Smith arrives, I think you're fine." Jonathan opened the door. "I, on the other hand, need to be going. Can we meet at the general store around noon for lunch? They serve a very nice soup-and-sandwich combo that's reasonably priced."

"Are you sure you're available?" Roberta felt her face burning. "I mean, I don't want anyone to get the wrong idea."

"Roberta, I am a totally free man to have lunch with anyone I choose to." He held out his arm. "May I walk with you to the post office? It's on the way to the lumber mill. If we walked separately, it would look like we don't care for each other's company."

"With that explanation, I'd be honored for you to show me the new post office." She was glad she'd put on a cotton shirtdress this morning, even if it was a little wrinkled. She'd worn the dress to work at her old job, so she figured it would be appropriate for running a post office. Besides, she only had one suit, and she'd been in it too many days already. She was sure the manual that Mr. Chase had given her would explain proper dress code for the job. As well as what she'd be paid and what she needed to do. Or at least she hoped so.

She didn't know what this new life held for her, but for right now, she was content to find out. And, she hadn't thought about Philip's betrayal since she stepped off the bus. Or at least not much.

After Jonathan left her at the post office, she walked through the empty rooms, trying to imagine what it might be like to actually work here full-time. There was an unfinished apartment in the back where she assumed Mr. Smith would live. She walked outside to the little patio, where a chair and table were already set up, and took a deep breath. This would be a perfect place for her new single life. If only Mr. Smith wasn't coming on the next bus.

Roberta put away any covetous thoughts about the too-perfect apartment. Mr. Chase had dropped off the mail that had come in from the bus driver, so she got busy sorting it and putting each envelope in its correct postal box.

Then she went to a basket that contained what appeared to be outgoing mail. There was a mail slot in the wall above it, and when she bent over to peer through it, an envelope came straight at her. "Oh," she gasped.

The depositor must have heard her. "Sorry if I scared you."

She leaned down again and opened the slot. She only saw a man's suited midriff in her view. Then his face filled the opening. She pulled back. It wouldn't do to have people talking about her being nosy about the mail coming into the post office. "That's okay.

I should be the one who's sorry. I'm just trying to figure out what I'm doing."

The man chuckled. "Aren't we all, dear girl? Aren't we all?"

Jonathan watched as Frank, the sawyer, positioned another log onto the carriage. First they'd cut the edges and bark off to make the log square, then they'd start cutting it into boards. The finer cuts would happen down the line. He and Frank made logs into a somewhat usable product. Pass after pass. The morning had gone smoothly. After seeing Roberta to the post office and making sure the key worked and the building was empty, he'd jogged to the lumber mill, clocking in just before time to start work. He joked around with a few of the younger guys, but the older, established workers didn't want to waste time chatting. Get in, do the work, then go home to their wives and children.

Cutting lumber was a hard job, and they had to be careful around the machines. The one he was assigned to had a nickname. The widow-maker. He rode the machine, watching for the new log to be rolled onto the saw carriage. He guessed since they knew he was single and just passing through, he'd drawn the short straw for machine assignments. It didn't bother him. He trusted Frank, his partner. That was a big part of being safe in dangerous jobs.

Jonathan had worked construction since he'd been in high school. His dad had insisted that his children learn the business from the ground up, so as soon as he could legally work in Chicago, he'd been cleaning up construction sites. He learned framing, plumbing, and finish work, and had apprenticed with an electrician the summer between his freshman and sophomore years of college. He'd enjoyed working with the electrician, but at the end of the summer he'd had to choose either going to trade school to learn the electrician craft or going back to college. It wasn't a hard choice. He'd gratefully returned to college that fall, combining the English classes he loved with the required business classes his father had insisted on.

His mom knew his true calling, but even she counseled him to get the business degree so his father would continue to pay for tuition and room and board. Taking business classes was the work part of school. Writing was the fun part. And when his father questioned his class load, Jonathan talked about the importance of clear writing for business contracts and documents. He didn't think he fooled his father, but at least he was able to graduate with a dual major.

He shook off the memories and focused on making sure the log was in position. If the log fell off, he wouldn't be the one hurt. He didn't want that on his conscience. He had enough regrets to take responsibility for.

He hummed a tune as he continued his work. He'd had a good session writing in his journal last night. He wrote about the bouncing kids getting off the bus and about their road-weary parents, but mostly he wrote about Roberta. Details he'd noticed, like the way she worried her bottom lip when she was trying to decide something. And about how strong she was to change her plans midstream to offer help when it was obviously needed.

He didn't write about how his heartbeat sped up just a little every time she looked at him. That was just a coincidence.

The smell of sawdust reminded him of the times he'd walked into the forest and sat under the pine trees that surrounded the town. It also reminded him of summers working with the construction crew.

In the middle of his musings, Frank called him down off the machine to help move a stuck log onto the carriage. "You're working hard today, Jonathan. Maybe you're trying to figure out how to make a home here in Deadwood with the lovely Constance Elliott."

"Frank, she's a child, not even out of high school yet. Besides, I know she's more interested in a boy she met at school. He's been coming around in the afternoons to study. I see them in the park." Jonathan smiled, thinking of sitting on the park bench later with Roberta. "I'm just doing my job."

"I've seen that look before on many a man's face." Frank shook his head. "It may not be the young Miss Elliott you're working for, but there's someone."

Jonathan pushed the log into place and climbed back up to his chair on the saw carriage. "I don't know what you're talking about."

Frank laughed. "Be that way. It's a small town. I'll know who it is by the end of the week at the latest. Then maybe I'll see if she'd rather have a strong, hard worker like me instead of a skinny runt like you."

"You're half my size," Jonathan reminded him as he adjusted the gears to get the log moving.

"Maybe, but I'm big in heart. Somehow, women see that and don't worry about my short stature." He raised his voice over the noise of the saw. "You better make your move soon, because I'm very attractive to women. I have a high-paying job, and I know how to dance."

"Well, you do sound like a catch. I'll tell this imaginary woman you're making up for me about you and your magnetism." His stomach growled, and he looked at his watch. "We have thirty minutes before the lunch bell. We need to focus on getting these logs finished. I don't want to be asked to work late."

When the lunch bell rang, he hurried over to the general store to meet up with Roberta. Frank and most of the other men brought their lunch in a tin pail. He'd found it easier just to pop into the general store and get a sandwich made. He looked around the room and didn't see Roberta. He went to talk to Mr. Chase and asked him if Roberta had been in that morning.

Mr. Chase grinned. "She came and left about thirty minutes ago."

Jonathan's heart sank. She'd forgotten about meeting him for lunch. "Well, I guess I better order a sandwich and get back to work."

"Do you mind taking Miss Stevens her lunch? She didn't get it when she stopped by this morning." He took a pail out from under the counter and set it on the table. "Please also let her know that her accommodations have been taken care of by the city treasurer. Her paycheck will be here each Friday. Honestly, I'm hoping she stays around. She's very nice."

Jonathan nodded. "Yes, she's very nice." And attractive. And smart. But those things he didn't say to Mr. Chase. Although he thought Mr. Chase somehow knew how he felt.

Back in Chicago, he'd dated in college. Mostly casual, group events, where it wouldn't be a one-on-one outing. He'd thought of asking a couple of women out, but he wasn't looking for a family. He wanted to explore. To visit Europe. And maybe even write a book.

"Jonathan, here's your sandwich and Miss Stevens's lunch. I threw in two orange sodas as well." Mr. Chase handed him the pail.

"And since you're being my delivery man today, no charge for your sandwich."

Jonathan took the pail. "That's very kind of you, but I'm going that way anyway. I can pay for my meal."

"I know you can. But you're doing me a favor. Can you also take this bundle of mail to Miss Stevens? It came in last week with the bus, and I haven't gotten around to even looking through it. I'm busier than a honeybee in spring." He pushed the package toward Jonathan. "I'm feeling bad about not getting these out to people earlier."

"Thank you for the sandwich. I'll get this right over to the post office." Jonathan looked at his watch. Ten minutes of his hour break were already gone. He hurried out of the store, waving at Amanda as she called his name. He knew he should stop and say hello, but he wanted to spend some time with Roberta and see how her day was going.

He held the door open for a woman with two children. Both were hanging on to her dress like they were afraid of what might be lurking in the store. Another description to write in his journal tonight—as long as he didn't use up today's page waxing poetically about Roberta and her red hair.

He grinned as he jogged toward the town square and the post office. The way he was feeling, all bets were off on what would actually show up on the page tonight.

CHAPTER FOUR

Jonathan found Roberta talking to a man and his son about the stamps she had available for purchase. She talked about the design of the stamps and the subject matter while they turned pages in the large catalog. "And if we don't have what you want, the manual says I can order a sheet and it will be here next week."

"Let's stick to what we came in for. Tommy mowed lawns for the neighborhood to make enough money for this purchase." The man nodded to his son. "Pay Miss Stevens, and we'll go home by way of the general store. I've got a couple of nickels we can spend on some of that maple syrup candy you love so much."

The boy, Tommy, counted out the money for the stamps as Roberta put them into a wax envelope. She took the change and then passed the envelope through the slot at the bottom of the cage divider that separated her from her customers. "Thank you for your business, and I'll order the next set so it's available when you're ready. You're going to have a wonderful collection."

"That's what we're hoping for. It's his college fund if we work it right." The man tousled his son's hair as they left the building.

"May I help you?" Roberta asked as she looked up. "Oh, sorry, Jonathan, I didn't see you there. What did you bring me?"

"Did you forget you were meeting me at the general store for lunch?" He held up the pail. "Since you didn't meet me, I brought lunch to you. And a pile of mail Mr. Chase found in the store."

She took the bundle of mail and then turned the sign on the door to closed. "Wait there for a minute. I'll put this in the back, and then we can go sit in the park to eat."

He glanced around the lobby area. Since this morning, Roberta had cleaned the windows, swept the floor, and restocked the booklets on the shelf. Someone had put the wanted posters up before Roberta came, and Jonathan studied them as he waited. The majority of the fugitives were murderers, but a few were accused of repeated grand theft.

He felt Roberta beside him before she said anything. He looked down, and she was reading the posters as well. He saw her shiver. "What's wrong?"

"I just can't imagine someone taking a life. Some of these men have taken more than one. How could you live with that?" She looked up at him, and Jonathan realized she expected an answer.

"Honestly, I don't know. I lived in Chicago where there's a mob of men who seem to enjoy killing people. Even those who aren't opposing them." He nodded to the door. "And on that happy note, let's go eat."

She followed him out, locking the door behind them. They strolled across the street to the square and sat at the first table they came across. "I can't believe how fun work was today. Did you know that we can sell money orders? You can send that money anywhere you want."

"I did know that." He handed her a sandwich and opened a bottle of the orange drink for her. She took the bottle and sighed. "What's wrong?" he asked.

"I only have this job until Mr. Smith arrives. I wish I could continue to work here. The manual says we'll eventually be delivering mail directly to the houses and that in addition to the postmaster job we need to hire a mail clerk and postal delivery men." She took a bite of the sandwich. After a moment she added, "But then I'd need to find a more permanent place to live, and, according to the manual, mail clerks don't make a lot of money. I'm not sure I could afford to live here when the city stops paying my expenses."

"One step at a time. Mr. Smith hasn't even arrived yet, and you're already planning your next move. Relax for a few days. Tell me about your morning. From the look of the lobby, you've been busy." He leaned back on the bench, watching her.

"It's been an interesting day so far. I expect a lot of my business was people who said they came in to check on mail when, really, they wanted to see the new girl in town. Did you know that, typically, even in a small town like this, mail gets delivered daily? It used to be twice a day, but they had to do some budget cuts. I'm learning a lot from the manual, in between sorting mail and selling three-cent stamps." She took another bite of her sandwich.

"I'm sure people are curious. It's not every day someone gets off the bus just to help out a stranger. I think you and I are the last two people to move here or even stop for more than a night in years. They want to get to know you."

Roberta focused on her sandwich. The bread was fresh and smelled like heaven. She was pretty sure if the people of Deadwood knew what happened to her at the church last month, they wouldn't want to get to know the girl whose fiancé chose to run away rather than marry her. She pinched the bridge of her nose. *Stop worrying about what people think,* she chided herself. Especially here. Here she could have a whole new past—all she had to do was claim it. Philip's betrayal could be a footnote on her biography. She set her sandwich down, half-eaten. "I'm not so sure about that."

Jonathan studied her for a minute. Then he reached over and squeezed her hand. "Everyone has secrets, Roberta. Today, you're right where you're supposed to be."

Roberta felt the tingle from her fingers all the way up her arm. She didn't want him to let go. On the other hand, what in the world was she doing? She had been about to marry another man a month ago. Now she was falling for an almost total stranger? Who was saying and doing all the right things. Just like Philip. She stood as soon as he moved his hand away. "I'm sorry, I'm very busy today. The citizens of Deadwood haven't had access to a real post office for a long time. I should get back to work."

"Roberta, I hope I wasn't being too forward," Jonathan said.

She could feel him standing behind her. She fixed a smile on her face and turned around. "Jonathan, we just don't know each other very well."

He handed her the pail containing the rest of her sandwich. "We do need to get to know each other. I'll be here at five to walk you to the boardinghouse. We could even sit in the park for a bit. I find it very restful. And a great place to talk and watch the good citizens of Deadwood."

"That's not what I meant." She hid her smile. "Now you're making fun of me."

"Not at all." But the grin on his face told a different story. "Have a nice afternoon, Roberta. I look forward to hearing about your day this evening."

She watched as he hurried back toward town where the mill must be located. She caught him looking over his shoulder at her, and her face heated. She quickly turned and marched to the post office where she could finish her lunch and think about what had just happened. "Jonathan Devons, you are a frustrating man," she said to the nearest tree.

A woman wiping a little girl's face nearby looked up at her. "Dear, all men are frustrating. It's the way God made them."

Roberta smiled as her face heated even more. "Your daughter is lovely."

"I wish she was a little less active. She'd rather run with her brothers than sit in the kitchen with me. But that's the way kids are, right?" She held out her hand. "I'm Sarah Morris. I'm the schoolteacher in town. When I'm not wrangling my own three. This is Jane. Say hello to Miss Stevens, Jane. She's our new postmistress. She brings us our mail."

Roberta tried not to look surprised that the woman already knew her name. "Actually, I'm only here temporarily." She took the child's outstretched hand. "Nice to meet you, Jane."

"I didn't know girls could deliver the mail. I wanted to ride the pony express, but Mama says they're all gone." Jane's eyes were wide with admiration.

"You know about the pony express?"

"We read a book about it. George said I couldn't be a rider, because I was a girl. But Mama said girls can do anything." Jane looked up at her mom. Then she sighed. "Except the pony express."

"Well, the post office took over for the pony express. Maybe you could work at a post office when you get older. It would kind of be the same thing," Roberta offered.

Jane sighed again, big and dramatic, as only a five-year-old child could do. "I don't want to deliver mail. I want to ride horses. And you don't ride horses to deliver mail now, right?"

"That's true. In fact, right now, while I'm waiting for the next postmaster to arrive, we aren't even delivering the mail. I get to sort it and wait for the person to come in and get it."

"That doesn't sound like fun at all. Mama, can I go look at the fountain?" Jane's attention had gone to the splashing water in the middle of the town square.

"No taking your shoes off and wading," Sarah called after Jane, who had taken off as soon as she'd asked permission. She turned and looked at Roberta. "That girl is a handful. She didn't mean to say your job is boring."

"It's not riding the pony express. I get it." Roberta glanced at her watch. "I probably should go reopen the office."

"I'd like to get to know you better. Would it be okay if I come by the boardinghouse one night this week and we can go for a walk about town? I'll tell you all the gossip." Roberta nodded, and Sarah started walking toward the fountain. "Especially the stuff about you."

Roberta watched her leave then realized what Sarah had said. She called after her, "What gossip about me?"

But if Sarah heard her, she didn't answer. Instead, she called to Jane, "Don't wade in the water with your shoes on either! Child, you're going to be the death of me."

Roberta left the mother and daughter to work it out and returned to the post office. She sat at the desk and tried to read more of the manual, but her brain was too full. She opened the desk drawers and found paper and an envelope. She took a pen and started writing a letter to her mother to let her know where she was and what she was doing.

She wrote, *Dear Mother, You'll never believe where my journey has taken me.*

After writing the letter, she sold herself a stamp and put the envelope into the outgoing mail.

Then she opened the packet that Jonathan had brought from Mr. Chase. Most of the items were newspapers. One of them was from New York. She opened the fold to find the mailing label and saw a photo of a painting she'd just seen in Mrs. Elliott's boardinghouse that morning. Shocked, she read the article.

Roberta glanced at the mailing label. It was to a Mrs. Thomas Gage. She recognized that name. She went into the back and saw there was a note in the Gages' box. She picked it up and read it aloud. "In light of Bea Gage's recent death, please forward all mail to Mrs. Gage's sister, Mrs. Wilfred Elliott."

Roberta sank into the nearest chair, floored at what she'd just found.

The painting she'd admired so much that morning had been stolen last month from a museum in New York City. Why did Mrs. Elliott have a stolen painting in her boardinghouse? Was that how she made enough money to take care of herself and her child?

She put the newspaper in Mrs. Elliott's box. She would deliver it to her landlady this evening along with a few questions. Maybe she should call the FBI? She went out to the lobby area and wrote the hotline number on a scrap of paper. Would they even be interested in a missing painting? She pondered the questions until a voice sounded behind her.

"Good afternoon. May I buy some stamps?" The man held three envelopes in his hand. He was dressed in a suit and wore a fedora, much like the one Mr. Smith had worn on the bus.

"I'm sorry, yes. Let me get back to the mail station and get those for you." Roberta stuffed the paper with the number of the FBI into her pocket. She'd decide what to do with it after she saw how Mrs. Elliott responded to hearing about the painting being stolen.

But, she mused as she pulled out the stamp book for the new customer, *why would she keep the painting on the wall where everyone could see it if she knew it was stolen*? That didn't make any sense at all.

"That will be nine cents. Do you want any stamps in particular?" She looked up into the man's face.

He smiled and took a dime out of his pocket. "As long as the letters get to Des Moines, I don't care if the stamps have jungle animals on them."

"I don't seem to have any jungle animals, but here's a set that commemorates the sesquicentennial of Washington, DC, as our capital. Do you have family in Des Moines?"

He shook his head. "It's just some business stuff. Jim Hooper, at your service. I'm the only lawyer within a two-hour drive, so if you have a dispute with anyone, come see me."

"I haven't gotten into any fights lately." She pushed the three stamps and his change toward him. "But you never know, the day's still young."

"I suppose a beautiful woman like you doesn't get in a lot of fights. You must have the men all fighting for your attention. What's your name?" He leaned on the counter, ignoring the stamps and the penny as he watched her.

"Roberta Stevens. For the time being, I'm stepping in for your postmaster." She pushed the stamps closer to him. "I don't think I'll have need for an attorney. I won't be around Deadwood that long."

"Now that's a shame." He picked up his stamps and change and tipped his hat. "Just remember I'm here if you need anything. I'm very knowledgeable about Deadwood history if you ever want a tour of the town."

Just then a woman stepped into the lobby. *Perfect timing.* Roberta smiled at her and waved her closer. "I can help you right here. Thanks for stopping in, Mr. Hooper."

Reluctantly, at least Roberta thought, Mr. Hooper stepped away from the service window and went to a large counter to put the stamps on his envelopes. After that, she had a steady stream of customers coming in to buy stamps or get a money order or just pick up their mail. Everyone introduced themselves, but, like Sarah, they already knew her name.

When the next woman asked for her mail, Roberta paused before going back to the sorting area. "How did you know my name?"

"Oh, Mr. Chase told me. He's been sending everyone who comes looking for mail or stamps over to meet you. He said you were a lovely young lady and, hopefully, our newest Deadwood resident.

If you do stay on, dear, I run a women's group out of the Methodist church over off Blaine Street. It's held every Wednesday evening, and we'd love to have you come visit us. Maybe even join."

Roberta glanced over to where Mr. Hooper had been standing, watching her. He'd left sometime during her rush. "Right now, my plans are a little vague. I was on my way to Portland when Mr. Chase asked me to do him this favor."

"Well, I'll tell you my opinion on Portland. I visited there last year to see my sister, and I couldn't find my way anywhere. You don't want to live in such a big city. Deadwood's just right. We have two churches, a general store, this post office, and soon a library. What more could you want?"

Roberta estimated that Mr. Chase must have sent every last soul in Deadwood into the post office that afternoon, and when she saw Jonathan walk in, she knew it was finally time to close up. She finished selling stamps to an older woman who liked writing letters to her family in South Dakota. She turned the sign on the door then called out to Jonathan, "I just need to check the back door and grab my purse, and I'll be with you."

She put the outgoing mail into a box in the large sorting room. Because Deadwood was so small, the manual said to hand off the outgoing mail to the next bus driver who arrived in town. Their post office was just a holding pen for the incoming and outgoing letters. Like the one to her mother. She hoped she would get a letter back before Mr. Smith arrived and it was time to leave Deadwood.

She swallowed the lump in her throat and went out to meet Jonathan. She had a lot of stories to tell the budding author. Maybe he'd find some of the people who visited her as inspiration for his own characters. It was nice to have someone to talk to, even if it was only a friendship.

She needed friends now. Probably more than ever. She put the newspaper and letter addressed to Mrs. Elliott in her purse. And maybe he'd be able to advise her on how to—or even if—she should approach their landlady about the painting. Maybe all Roberta really needed to do was drop off the newspaper. That way no one would want to kill the messenger.

At least she hoped.

❧ CHAPTER FIVE ❧

Jonathan pointed to a park bench as they walked through the town square. "Let's sit for a minute. We have time before dinner is served. You look stressed. What happened this afternoon? You were excited about the job at lunch."

Roberta sighed as she nearly fell onto the bench. She tried to formulate her thoughts into a coherent stream. So much had happened. She decided to address her emotions first, since they might overwhelm her. Philip had told her to ignore her uneasy feelings every time she'd questioned their relationship. Which, now that she thought about it, should have been a big red flag. But Jonathan wasn't Philip. "First thing, I'm really loving working here, and it hit me this afternoon that no matter how much I read the manual or set up Deadwood's mail system, as soon as Mr. Smith arrives, he's the one who decides if I get to stay or not."

"You're thinking about staying?" Jonathan smiled as he leaned against the bench.

"That's what you deduced from my pouring out my concerns?" Roberta pressed her face into her hands. Maybe talking about this with Jonathan was a bad idea.

"No, I heard a lot in that statement. I'm just reacting to the part that makes me happiest. You don't know that Mr. Smith will even show up, much less refuse to hire you." He leaned forward, resting his arms on his knees. "Didn't you tell me he was kind when you met him on the bus? I don't think a kind man is going to throw you out of work just because you did an amazing job."

"I know it's emotion that's pushing that button, but the concern is still there. He might have already hired his staff. So even if he wants to hire me, he can't." She pulled the newspaper from her purse. "Let's let that go. On to problem number two. Look at that painting and tell me if you recognize it."

He unfolded the paper. "This is a New York paper. Where did you get it?"

"Mrs. Elliott's sister had a subscription. There was a note in her box that said to give anything for Bea Gage to Mrs. Elliott, so I'm taking it home to her. When I opened it to see if there was an address label on the paper, I saw that picture."

He squinted at the paper. "That's the painting you were admiring this morning in the hallway."

"I believe so. That paper is a month old. Mr. Chase must have had that pile stuck behind something at the store."

Jonathan frowned. "If this is a stolen painting and it's the one in her house, she needs to know."

"Jonathan, what if she already knows?" Roberta let the implication settle.

"No, I can't believe that. She has a daughter in the house. Not to mention all of us. She wouldn't put it up on display if she knew." He stood and held out his hand. "Let's go talk to our landlady."

Roberta let Jonathan pull her to her feet. His hand was rough from working at the lumber mill, and strong. Not something she should be thinking about right now as they were discussing stolen merchandise.

Jonathan grinned at her as they hurried to the house. "Before you moved here, Deadwood was a really quiet little town. Now it's exciting, and I'm going to have a lot to write about tonight in my journal. Thanks for stirring the pot."

"All I did was recognize a famous painting," Roberta reminded him. Right now, she wished she didn't have such a good eye for authentic pieces of art. Then she could have bought a new drawing pad and pencils at the general store and been drawing this evening. Now she was going to have to decide if Mrs. Elliott was a thief or at least knowingly in possession of stolen property.

He held the front door to the boardinghouse open, and Roberta followed him to the kitchen, where she knew they'd find Mrs. Elliott putting the final touches on dinner. Tonight's meal was soup and fresh rolls. Roberta's stomach growled at the smell of the rolls baking in the oven.

Mrs. Elliott looked up from the stove. "Well, don't you two look determined? What can I help you with?"

Jonathan nodded to the kitchen table. "Can we sit down a minute?"

"Of course, go right ahead. I take it you need dinner early?" She reached for a couple of bowls.

"No, we don't need to eat early. Please, come sit with us," Roberta said as she slipped onto a chair. She waited for the obviously confused Mrs. Elliott to sit in the chair between them before nodding to Jonathan.

He unfolded the paper and pushed it across the table. "Roberta found this in your sister's mail."

Roberta pulled out the letter she'd brought home for her land-lady and slid it toward her as well. "This also came for you. But we're here to talk about the painting."

Mrs. Elliott frowned at the painting on the front page. "It says this painting was stolen from a New York art museum. That can't be the same painting I have in the hallway. I've had that one for about a month."

"Look at the date of the paper. It's been sitting around a while," Roberta pointed out. "I think that painting you have is the original that was stolen last month. The brushstrokes are in the artist's style. I took a class studying this era of paintings in school."

"Albert sent the painting to Bea. And if this is stolen…" Mrs. Elliott pressed her hand to her mouth. When she got back in control of her emotions, she sighed. "He always wanted an easy way to get rich. We need to reach out to the museum and see if this is theirs."

"Wait, you think your sister was the one who was supposed to get the painting?" Roberta was confused.

"My sister, Bea Gage, received that package last month. I assumed that her son, my nephew, Albert, sent it for her birthday. Mr. Chase gave it to me after she passed. I had most of her mail sitting here on my desk, and I spilled some water on the parcel. I opened it to see what was inside, and I'm glad I did. The water could have ruined the canvas." She went over to the counter, opened a drawer, and pulled out some brown wrapping paper. "I couldn't really tell what the return address said—but doesn't it look like an A. Gage? And the city is definitely New York City. The last Bea told me was that Albert was living the high life out there. We tried to reach him at the address she had in her book, but the letter was returned a week after the funeral. If you see any mail to Bea, please bring it to me. I'd like to let her only child know that she's gone."

Jonathan and Roberta shared a glance. Mrs. Elliott wasn't the thief. But maybe her sister had knowingly taken stolen goods and held them for her son. It was a long shot, and Roberta thought it was more likely that Albert had used his mother, but Bea's involvement couldn't be overlooked.

"Mrs. Elliott, maybe your sister has another address for her son at her house. One you didn't find," Jonathan said. Roberta noticed that he didn't mention the fact that Bea might also have other paintings that were of questionable origin. "Could Roberta and I go over to her house tonight and check it out? Then we should call the sheriff about securing the painting. I'd hate to see your nephew come here looking for the painting. Or send someone to get it. Especially with Constance here."

Now Mrs. Elliott looked fierce. She stood, marched over to the wall, and came back with a key from the hanger by the door. "You better go now while there's light," she said, handing it to him. "I had the utilities turned off at the house until we could find Albert. No use in racking up a bill that no one can pay."

He took the key, standing as he pocketed it. "Mrs. Elliott, are you sure your sister didn't know?"

"She wouldn't have done this. Her husband, Thomas, would have helped Albert, but he's been gone for years. He was shot on a business trip to Portland when Albert was eight. There were rumors...." Mrs. Elliott brushed away tears. "But Bea wasn't like that. She was straight as an arrow. I know it."

Roberta stood. "Thank you. We'll return as soon as we can."

"Soup and rolls will reheat if you miss dinner." Mrs. Elliott folded the paper. "The only good part of this is that Bea's gone. She worshipped that boy. This would have broken her heart."

As they left the boardinghouse, Roberta glanced back and saw Mrs. Elliott had followed them out to the front porch and was now sitting in one of the rockers, watching them. She turned to Jonathan. "She's taking this better than I expected."

"Mrs. Elliott is the salt of the earth. She's gone through some bad times before, and she's come out of it stronger." He nodded toward the town square. "We need to go this way and then turn on Baker Street. The house is on the end of the street."

"How do you know that?" Roberta realized they hadn't even asked Mrs. Elliott where her sister's home was located.

"I went over to the house with Constance a week ago to check on everything. I think Mrs. Elliott was trying to start a romance, but the girl is too young for me. Besides, she already has a boyfriend. They just haven't told anyone. You know, young love." He laughed. "Mrs. Elliott was a little put out when I told her I wasn't looking for a wife. She eased up on me when I told her I was engaged up until recently and needed some time to clear my head from that."

Roberta tried not to look at Jonathan. Her heart was pounding in her chest. What if his situation was the same as hers? What if he'd been left at the altar? "You were engaged?"

"My father set it up right after I graduated from college. When I left Chicago, I broke off the engagement." He pointed to the upcoming street. "There's where we need to turn."

Roberta walked in silence next to him. He'd been the one to leave. Like Philip. Was there a good reason? Or was it just about him? Now she didn't know what to think about the charming Mr. Jonathan Devons. She swallowed a lump in her throat. Why was she reacting this way? They were acquaintances, barely friends. He didn't owe her any kind of explanation.

The house was cute, nestled in the trees at the end of the block. Nothing special about the construction, but it had been kept up well. At least, Jonathan assumed, until its resident had died. Now it was beginning to show signs of neglect. It was like the house knew it was alone. That no one loved it anymore. Jonathan's dad used to laugh at him when he personalized inanimate objects, telling him to grow up. But his mother had encouraged his imagination from the start. Why was it that his mother could see the potential in him, but his father just wanted him to fit the mold of a good son?

He glanced over at Roberta, who seemed to be just as lost in her thoughts as he was in his. Would she understand if he told her what he saw? He was about to say something when she turned to him.

"We probably better get inside before we lose the light." She pointed to the setting sun. Deadwood didn't have streetlamps yet, not like Chicago.

Jonathan took out the key and walked over to unlock the house. When he opened the door, the air from the interior smelled dusty and stale. He swung his arm in invitation. "After you."

Roberta walked through the door and straight to a painting on the wall. "This can't be."

"What is it?" Jonathan was afraid of what she was going to say.

Instead of answering, she looked around the room. Then she pointed at four additional paintings. "I'm not an expert, but I think we need to get someone in here to look at all of these paintings."

"You think they're stolen?"

Roberta nodded and continued to examine the paintings. After a few minutes she said, "I believe that Albert Gage was using his mother as a storage facility for his stolen art."

When they got back to the boardinghouse, dinner was just about over. They took their meal in the kitchen where Mrs. Elliott could talk. Roberta had made a list of the paintings, and she went over them as Mrs. Elliott tried to recall when her sister had received each one.

Finally, Mrs. Elliott stopped washing dishes and sat down at the table with them. Jonathan felt bad for the woman. She looked like someone had taken her favorite book and shredded it in front of her. "This is really happening, isn't it?" she asked them.

When Jonathan nodded, she leaned back in her chair. "Bea was so happy that Albert had taken up an interest in art. Bea always loved art. She was always drawing something. But girls didn't go to school for drawing. Our parents arranged Bea's marriage first, and she did what she was told. I informed my folks that I wanted to marry Wilfred so they better not make any different arrangements. I wonder how much my life would have been different if I had let them decide."

Mrs. Elliott sighed. Then she looked at the clock on the wall. "Give me thirty minutes to make sure the boarders are in their rooms. I'll send Constance up as well. Then I'll meet you in the parlor, and we can call the sheriff. We don't have actual police here in

Deadwood. We're serviced by the Lane County Sheriff's Office in Eugene. That's an hour away. So we won't see anyone until tomorrow, probably. Especially since this isn't an emergency. So now, you two need to eat. You've hardly touched your potato soup. It was my mother's recipe, but I added the egg dumplings. It makes it filling, yet Gerald still wants his loaf of bread and butter on the table. Even with the rolls."

She left the kitchen, and Jonathan took a bite of his soup and then buttered his roll. He didn't look over at Roberta when he addressed her. "She's still trying to take care of others, when her heart must be broken. It's a good thing you decided to take a bus to Portland. You might have just saved a few lives as well as returning those paintings to their rightful owners."

When she didn't answer him, he looked up. He reached for her hand across the table, but she moved it to her lap. "Roberta? Is everything okay? You're not worried about someone coming to get the paintings, are you? It's almost over. We just need to talk to the sheriff tonight, and he'll take over."

"I'm fine. I'm just a little tired. It's been an exhausting day." She picked up her spoon and started eating.

The one thing Jonathan knew about woman was that when they said they were fine, most of the time they weren't. He'd said something that upset her, but for the life of him he couldn't figure out what that might be. He knew a second thing about women. It was better not to push unless you wanted a fight. And right now, they had bigger things on their plate.

He ate his dinner, and neither one of them talked again until Mrs. Elliott came back into the kitchen.

"It took a while. Gerald wanted to read the paper in the parlor, but I told him I wasn't feeling well and wondered if he might read in his room."

"Are we ready to call the sheriff then?" Roberta asked, not meeting anyone's gaze.

"Let's go into the parlor where we can shut the doors." Mrs. Elliott led the way, and Roberta followed.

Jonathan watched the women leave. Yes, there was definitely something different about Roberta this evening. She wasn't the same person she'd been at lunchtime. However, they might have uncovered an art theft ring, so he'd give her some space. At least until tomorrow. She was still planning on leaving when the elusive Mr. Smith arrived. If he was on the bus, he was only a few days away. He needed to get her to see that staying wouldn't be that bad of an idea. For either of them.

CHAPTER SIX

Jonathan walked Roberta to the post office the next morning. "I can't believe the deputy told us he'd tell the sheriff when he got back. Like he's busy chasing down bank robbers or murderers. Seriously, this situation is a danger to Mrs. Elliott, her daughter, and anyone else, like you and me, who lives in that house. What if some mobster comes in the middle of the night for the paintings? Maybe we should call again this morning and see if we can get someone else on the line who knows what he's doing."

"I guess we should make sure we lock our doors. I'm sure the message will be passed on to whoever is in charge while the sheriff is away." Roberta seemed more normal today. Not lost in thought like she had been last night. Whatever had been bothering her had been either lightened or washed away with the new day.

"You need to take this seriously. We're in real danger." Jonathan dodged a kid running down the street toward the school, pulling Roberta out of the way at the same time.

"I think we're in danger of being run over by kids here on the street." Roberta laughed as he frowned at her. "I have a plan B. I'll call the museum in New York and tell them I might know where their missing painting is located, and they'll get ahold of their FBI contact. Someone has to care about the missing art."

"You didn't just think about this, did you?" Jonathan was impressed with her ability to zigzag when she needed to.

"Nope. The deputy might call before the sheriff gets back, but he was pretty solid that he couldn't open an investigation without talking to his boss. So reaching out to the museum might get someone on it sooner."

"Well, I'm glad you thought about a plan B. I'm just standing here griping. What time do you want to eat lunch?" He paused at the post office door and waited for her answer.

"You don't have to—"

"Nope." Jonathan shook his head. "I'm eating lunch with you and walking you to and from work until they figure out if those paintings were stolen. Who knows, Albert might just be really good at picking out copies and sending them at the most inopportune times."

Roberta smiled, and his heart pounded. He was falling hard. What was he going to do if Smith showed up on Friday? Leave and follow her? Would that look desperate? Right now, he didn't care. He wasn't going to let this woman out of his life. Even though they hadn't made any promises to each other or even gone on a real date yet. "So, what time?"

She bit her lip again, pondering her answer.

She was so cute when she did that.

"I'd rather eat at one, if possible. Yesterday's afternoon session was long and filled with customers. If I break it up with lunchtime, it'll give me more time to get things done in the morning." She smiled at him. "Thanks for walking me to work."

"Thanks for being such an amazing art expert." He waved and strolled toward Deadwood Lumber and his job. "Mona Lisa," by Nat King Cole, came into his head. The song was perfect. Roberta was his own Mona Lisa. Especially with that smile she gave him sometimes. He hummed all the way to the mill.

Roberta opened the post office and took the bundle of incoming mail to the sorting room. According to the manual, she had thirty minutes to sort before she had to open the customer window at eight thirty. Which was plenty of time to call the art museum. She'd written down a tip line number from the article last night on a piece of scrap paper that she'd shoved into her pocket when she'd gotten dressed that morning. She settled at the large desk in the postmaster's office and picked up the phone. Then she dialed the operator and asked to be connected to the number on the paper.

It took several clicks and whirls, but soon she heard a voice on the line. "John Carver speaking."

"Hello, is this the New York Art Museum?"

"Yes, ma'am, but this is the fraud office. You'll need to call the general number for our open hours."

"Actually, you're just the person I need to talk to," Roberta hastened to say. "I just read the article about last month's theft, and I think the Butler landscape is here in Deadwood, Oregon."

"Excuse me?" The man sounded flustered.

Roberta repeated what she'd said, and then she explained how the painting came to be hanging on a boardinghouse wall in a small mountain town. "Can you send someone to look at it? And collect it? The owner of the boardinghouse is concerned about having a stolen painting in her possession."

"What is your name again? Can you give me a good number to call you back? I need to talk to my FBI contact and my supervisor to see when we could arrive. I'm sure it can't be before Monday. Are you or the boardinghouse owner in any danger?"

"Not that I can tell, but you never know. We don't know if the person who sent the paintings is going to come for them or not. Either way, we need to get them back to the museum, right?" Roberta glanced at the clock. She only had ten minutes before she needed to open the window, and she hadn't checked the manual for her daily list. It might not be her forever position, but she still wanted to do a good job. She gave the man her name and the phone number to the post office. Then she told him she needed to go and hung up.

Roberta wrote down John Carver's name in the Monday block on the calendar. She was relieved she'd been able to reach someone who cared about the paintings. Of course, she'd forgotten to tell him about the other paintings in Bea Gage's house. But she'd said "paintings"—plural—maybe he'd heard that. She'd give him the list on Monday. Which would give her an excuse to stay a few more days in case Mr. Smith arrived on Friday.

She pushed the what-ifs and possibilities out of her head and worked on sorting the mail.

Later that morning, Mr. Hooper came into the post office again. Instead of getting in line, he leaned against the back wall and waited for the lobby to empty out. When they were alone, he strolled up to the cage and smiled at her. "Good morning, Roberta."

"Mr. Hooper, how can I help you?"

He held his hand against his heart. "I'm hurt that you don't remember my first name."

Roberta raised her eyebrows. "I remember it. I choose not to use it. Now, I'm very busy, so if this is nothing but a friendly visit, I must be going."

"You are very dedicated to your job," he said, and his eyes twinkled, like he didn't really mean the words. "I'm here to invite you to lunch. Before you say no, I know you have to eat. I'd love to learn more about you. Where you're from. How you got here. Those types of subjects."

"I'm sorry, but I've already got a date for lunch. Maybe another time." Roberta turned to go into the back.

"What about dinner or lunch tomorrow? It would just be a casual get-to-know-you meal. No pressure. No expectations. If we find out we're not compatible, I'll leave you alone. It's not every day a beautiful woman is dropped off a bus in Deadwood. I just don't want to lose my chance." He smiled again.

Roberta calculated the pros and cons. Finally, she said, "Lunch tomorrow. At one o'clock. And you're buying. Where do you want to meet?"

He grinned. "I admire your optimism. Besides the general store that sells sandwiches, there's only one other place to eat. Annie's Café. I'll meet you there at one."

Roberta watched as he walked out. The man was nothing if not confident. Probably because of his profession. In a way, he reminded her of Philip. Philip had looked like Jonathan, with his dark rugged looks, but acted more like Mr. Hooper. Jim. Since she was letting him buy her lunch, she probably should call him by his first name.

Sarah Morris walked into the office with Jane. "Was that Jim Hooper I saw coming out of here just now? He's probably the most eligible and richest bachelor in Deadwood. Not only is he a lawyer, but his family owns a large cattle ranch outside of town. You need to sign that contract, missy."

"I'm not signing any contract. And I'm not looking for a man to marry. I've got a job to do here." Roberta smiled down at Jane. "And what are you doing today? Riding the pony express or being the engineer on a train?"

Jane brightened. "I hadn't thought about running a train. I could do that, right, Mama?"

"Of course you can. Now go outside and wait on the step until I get done with my business with Miss Stevens, okay?" Sarah brushed her daughter's hair out of her eyes.

They watched as Jane skipped out the door. Then Sarah turned back to Roberta. "Now, dear, you can't be serious. You're not looking for a husband?"

"Sarah, I don't even know if I'm going to be here next week." Roberta glanced around the post office lobby, which was quickly feeling like home. She'd need to sweep the floors tonight before she closed up. Bob Smith was a lucky man to be stationed here in Deadwood. She wondered if he realized it. "Anyway, I'd love to still take a walk and chat one of these nights. Are you available tonight or tomorrow night?"

"Friday night is the town social and cake walk at the Methodist church. Why don't you come? Most of the town will be there, no matter where they attend or what they believe."

"That sounds like fun. I'd love to come." On the one hand, Roberta was a little hesitant to make more ties to Deadwood and its residents. Especially since she'd probably be in Portland by next week. But on the other hand, maybe she could find out more about Bea Gage and her wayward son. John Carver, the art museum guy, had called and said to expect them on Monday. She told them to meet her at the post office. She hoped she'd still be working there.

"Do I need to bring a cake?"

"That would be wonderful if you could. I'll understand, though, if it doesn't work out. I know you're staying at the boardinghouse. Maybe Mrs. Elliott would let you use her kitchen after dinner."

"Mama," Jane called from the doorway, "the bells are ringing for twelve o'clock. Don't we need to go to the store?"

"And I'm being called back to my chores. I'll see you at the Methodist church at seven on Friday. You might want to come a little early to drop off your cake." Sarah waved as she left the office.

Roberta looked around. She had an hour before Jonathan would be there with her lunch. She had so much to tell him. She wandered to the sorting room to make sure all the mail was where it needed to be and to check the daily list the manual provided for things to do. Maybe he'd like to attend the cake walk with her?

She mused about the type of cake she could make and what she'd need from the store to make one. She would talk to Mrs. Elliott tonight. It had been a while since she'd felt like baking.

Jonathan was trying to focus on his work when the first break was called. Frank handed him a cup of coffee. "Didn't you get enough sleep last night?"

"Does it show?" Jonathan took the cup gratefully.

Frank nodded. "Yup. You're not as precise today. Something you want to talk about? Like maybe that new gal over at the post office?"

"So rumors are starting, huh?" Jonathan grinned.

"A few. Of course, it doesn't help that your landlady is Roland's sister." Frank leaned on a pallet of stacked boards.

"I have to admit, I'm attracted to Roberta." He rubbed the back of his neck. "That's not what's keeping me awake at night though."

"Not the gal then. One thing before we change the subject, you need to remember that the first week you were here, all you could talk about was your next stop. I haven't heard you say anything about leaving since Monday." Frank met Jonathan's gaze and held it.

"That's true." Jonathan thought about his plans. Monday, he'd been thinking about leaving Deadwood, if not Friday, then the next Friday. Now? He wasn't sure he wanted to leave at all. At least, not if Roberta decided to stay. "I guess I'm just taking that one day at a time."

"So what has you worried?" Frank asked.

"What do you know about Albert Gage?" Jonathan lowered his voice, just in case Roland was nearby. He didn't want Mrs. Elliott hearing that he'd been looking into her nephew.

"The Gage boy? He was trouble right up to the time he left home after dropping out of school at sixteen. His mama worshipped him, but he didn't have a man around to do the hard stuff, like discipline. Always in trouble, that one. I hate to see our young folks leave town when they grow up, but he was an exception." Frank glanced around again. "Just don't mention what I said to Roland, since Albert's his nephew too."

"That's kind of what I got from Mrs. Elliott, so I'm sure it wouldn't be a shock to Roland." Jonathan was beginning to get a picture of what kind of man would send his mother stolen goods to hold. "I guess he hasn't been here for a while?"

"Not for two, maybe three years. Then he visited his mama, stayed the night, and left the next day. From what I heard, he took back a few of the gifts he'd sent her, saying he needed to sell them for another investment." Frank glanced at his watch. "We better get moving again or Roland's going to find someone younger to take our jobs."

"I'm not old, you are," Jonathan teased as he stood and reached for Frank's cup. "I'll take these to the break room."

As the morning wore on, Jonathan mused on the paintings and the next step. He wondered if Roberta had any luck with the art museum. They needed to get that painting out of the boardinghouse to protect Mrs. Elliott and Constance. Maybe they could store all the paintings at the general store or the post office. Somewhere public. Just in case Albert Gage decided to come and get a painting or two from the makeshift vault he'd created at his mother's.

Once the painting issue was handled, he was going to take Roberta for a ride to see the waterfall and the land in the canyon he'd found. The owner was one of the guys who sold logs to the mill, and he'd offered Jonathan a great deal on the patch. The logging off the flat area had been mostly completed, and it was ready to build a house on or be turned into a pasture for livestock or both.

Maybe he should take him up on the offer. He had his trust money. Even if he didn't build or do anything with the land, he'd have someplace to come back to once this time of wandering was done. He wasn't ever returning to Chicago, no matter how much his mother begged.

No, buying something out here would be an investment in his future. A future with or without Roberta. But it would be nice to hear what she thought of the idea. She had a good head on her shoulders. She had plans for her life. Jonathan was just hoping that he could convince her to adjust them. She'd still be in Oregon, just not Portland. And the post office was a good job. Probably much better than what she'd have to start with at a corporation in Portland. His family business had seen its share of female workers, at least in the office. Most of them didn't stay for long. They got married and left. Roberta didn't seem like the type to quit her job just for a guy.

And in his opinion? That was too bad.

Chapter Seven

A solitary lunch pail sat on the counter when he arrived at the general store. Mr. Chase handed him a bundle of mail and pointed at the bucket. "I thought you'd be in earlier."

"Roberta, I mean, Miss Stevens, asked to eat at one rather than straight-up noon. I should have stopped by to tell you this morning." He took the bundle from Mr. Chase. "More lost mail?"

"Tell her I'm sorry. I didn't realize I had this bundle as well. I've looked all around the office, and it's the last one." He tapped the bundle in Jonathan's hands. "I glanced through it, and there's a letter to Bea Gage. Can you make sure Mrs. Elliott gets that today? It might be a condolence letter, but if it isn't, I'd hate for someone close not to know she'd passed on."

"I'll remind Miss Stevens to take it to the boardinghouse tonight. What do I owe you for my lunch?" He reached into his pocket for his money clip.

"No charge today, since you're helping me out by delivering the mail. Don't worry about it. I'll charge you for your lunch when I'm not using you as a pack mule." Mr. Chase waved at him and then went to help a customer.

"Thank you." Jonathan picked up the bucket and moved to leave the store.

"Mr. Devons," Amanda called, "I want to ask you something."

He paused at the counter. "Good afternoon, Amanda. I'm in a bit of a hurry, sorry."

"I just wanted to see if you're going to the Methodist social on Friday. You're more than welcome," she said.

"Thank you for the opportunity, but I've got other plans." He felt bad now about even talking to her when he first arrived. He could see how she would think he was interested in taking their relationship further. He'd been lonely and needed someone to talk to after work. And Amanda read a lot.

Now he felt like a heel. But, if he was going to choose and put all his eggs in one basket, so to speak, it was going to be Roberta, not Amanda. He said goodbye and tried to ignore the disappointment that registered on the young woman's face.

Frank had been willing to change his lunchtime, but Roland had made it clear it was a one-time adjustment. The guys in the yard needed to have an ongoing stream of boards to make the time productive. When Jonathan had worked for his family business, his comings and goings weren't watched as closely as they were here, where he was a cog in the production line. When he was late, the line didn't start. When he left early, the line stalled.

If he and Roberta were going to continue to have lunch together, they needed to go back to noon, since quitting his job wasn't an option. Not if he wanted to stay in Deadwood.

He hurried to the post office and found Roberta standing outside, waiting for him. He smiled and held up the bundle of mail. "Do you want to put this inside before you lock up?"

"Oh no. Mr. Chase found another one?" She pulled out her key and opened the door. Then she took the bundle and set it inside on the counter where she'd see it when she returned. Coming back outside, she relocked the door. "I wanted to be waiting for you. I know you don't have much time for lunch."

"I have to have lunch at noon starting tomorrow. It upsets the flow at the mill if I take it at one." He nodded to a bench, and they sat down. He opened the pail and handed her a sandwich then took out the bottles so he could open them. "We need to return Mr. Chase's lunch pails to him. Maybe tonight after work?"

"Let's do that. I'll clean everything up and gather the bottles together this afternoon." She took a bite of her sandwich. "I've got news."

"About the post office or the paintings?" He studied her. She looked happy.

"The paintings. The art museum and the FBI are sending someone to come evaluate the one at the boardinghouse and take it back if it's really the stolen one. I thought the museum man was going to hang up on me when I first called, but he finally listened. We'll have them take the other paintings also." She broke off a piece of bread from her sandwich and tossed it to a waiting pigeon. "I'll be in town at least until Monday. No matter what Mr. Smith decides."

"That's wonderful." He couldn't hide his grin. "I should take you around tonight. That way, you'll know what you're leaving."

She looked around the town square. "Honestly, with our trip to Bea Gage's house last night, I think I've seen most of the town."

"It's the surrounding area I want to show you. Come take a drive with me. We can drop Mr. Chase's things off then go back to the boardinghouse to get my car. Maybe Mrs. Elliott can put our dinner in a basket and we can eat while we're gone?" His mouth went dry as he waited for her answer. Or it could have been from the sandwich. Either way, he took a sip of soda before he continued. "I have this place I'd love to show you. And you need to see the waterfall."

She smiled. "Well, how could I refuse?"

"It's a date then." He dug into his sandwich and ignored the shocked look on Roberta's face at his use of the word.

After a few minutes of silence, she asked, "So how was your morning?"

"We cut boards. A lot of boards. It's really not all that interesting. The guys are terrific. Frank, he's the guy I work with the most, has been in Deadwood for years. Probably at the mill for as long as he's been in town. He's solid and easy to talk to. Roland Farmer is the foreman who hired me. He's Mrs. Elliott's brother. Did I tell you that already?"

"Maybe. I think I've heard it before. You don't love your job?"

He paused before he answered. "I don't hate it. I feel like I'm doing my part to expand the area. Making boards so they can be made into houses, churches, and towns. It's like I'm helping to expand civilization. Maybe the stonemasons for the pyramids felt the same way."

Roberta laughed. "Well, that's one way to look at it. Have you been doing any writing at night? I'm afraid I'm taking up all your writing time."

"Don't worry about it. I wouldn't ask you to do things with me if I didn't want to be with you." Jonathan glanced into the pail. "It looks like Mr. Chase sent along two cookies. I'm taking it that you don't want one?"

"Are you crazy? Why wouldn't I want a cookie?" As he laughed, she grabbed the pail and retrieved the cookies. "Just for that, I'm taking the bigger one."

Roberta loved having lunch with Jonathan. When it was just the two of them, she felt more comfortable talking about her feelings, her fears, and even sometimes her hopes and dreams. When she'd made her demand on what time to have lunch, she'd never even thought of the effect it might have on his job. That was so unlike her. She was usually the giver in a relationship. The one who always changed her plans to fit others' needs. What had gotten into her? Could she have changed so much in such a short period of time?

Whatever it was, she liked the stronger, more confident Roberta.

She took the newest bundle and, before opening the customer window, quickly sorted it. When she came to the letter to Mrs. Gage, she put that into her purse along with another letter to Mrs. Elliott. She'd drop those off when they went to get dinner and Jonathan's car.

Pleased with her progress, she moved back to the front and opened the window. No one was in the lobby, so she went to the desk and took out three pieces of paper. On the top of the first one, she wrote *Weekly Tasks*. Then she made sheets for daily and monthly tasks. She didn't see any that were annual or semiannual yet, so she took out a fourth piece and set it aside, just in case.

The manual was set up for a larger post office in a much larger town. The building had been built with growth in mind, so there were several empty offices, a conference room, and a large break room. Since she was the only one here, she mostly used the sorting room for everything unless she was out front. Then she used the middle service window. There were three of them. She liked the symmetry of using the middle one. Of course, once there was more than one clerk, she'd probably want them to use the two outside windows, but that wouldn't be her decision. Right now, all she could concentrate on was what she could control. And getting a system set up for Mr. Smith was her first priority. He could use it or throw it away when he arrived, but setting it up kept her busy. And she was learning more and more about running a post office. If she did go to Portland, maybe they'd have a place for someone who'd read the manual and was already knowledgeable. She'd ask Mr. Smith for a reference.

The afternoon went by fast. She closed the doors at four thirty so she could sweep and mop the front area. She returned the mop and now empty bucket to the closet that held all the cleaning supplies. Then she checked the clock, retrieved her things, and closed the office for the night, leaving by the back door.

She'd finished all the items on the daily to-do list and one of the items on the weekly list. She'd drawn out a calendar and had put *lobby floor* on every Wednesday square. She rolled her shoulders, hoping the knots would release just a little, and walked around the building to meet Jonathan out front.

Instead, Jim Hooper stood there. He must have tried the door because now he was pressing his face against the glass she'd just cleaned and looking inside the empty lobby.

"We'll be open again in the morning at eight thirty, Mr. Hooper," Roberta called from the bottom of the stairs.

"Oh, there you are, Miss Stevens. I was wondering if you would have dinner with me. I know we said lunch tomorrow, but I was walking by and wondered if you were free." He hurried down the stairs to where she was standing.

"I'm sorry, I have dinner plans," she said. Somehow it felt like an excuse, but it was true. She'd told Jonathan she'd go with him. On the tour of Deadwood that Mr. Hooper had offered several days ago. "And since you're here, I'm afraid I'm going to have to cancel lunch plans as well. I've got a lot of work to do."

His eyes flashed what looked like anger for a second but could have been surprise. If he was well-known as a rich, eligible bachelor, no one probably ever said no to him. And yet, Roberta had, three— no, four—times now. The guy couldn't be happy.

"I'm sorry to hear that. I'd be glad to bring over lunch for you so you didn't have to leave. Like the worker from the mill is doing." His gaze told her that he knew Jonathan and that he didn't approve of Roberta's choice of suitors. The good news was he wasn't in charge of her or who she saw.

"That's okay. I actually have my lunch delivery set up. Now, if you'll excuse me, I'm waiting for someone." She glanced around the town square but didn't see Jonathan coming.

"I can wait with you." He sat on one of the close benches and patted the seat next to him. "I'm sure we'll find something to talk about, even if it's just the lovely weather Deadwood has been having this week."

"Seriously, you don't have to wait with me. I have a book to read." She patted her purse, hoping she'd actually brought a book this morning.

"I can wait. Besides, I think tonight's date is actually coming up the path right now. Oh my, he's covered with sawdust. You'll probably be delayed while he cleans up." Mr. Hooper nodded toward the sidewalk where Jonathan was walking their way. He didn't look happy.

Roberta was glad she hadn't sat down now. It might look like she was interested in Mr. Hooper's attention. Which she definitely wasn't. And she'd been as clear on that as possible, with the one slipup of accepting his lunch offer. She'd corrected that today, and yet he was still here.

Jonathan arrived and stood next to her. "Miss Stevens, are you ready to go to the general store?"

"I've got everything here." She looked at Jim Hooper. "Mr. Hooper was just keeping me company while I waited for you."

"How nice of him. I was kept a little late at work." He reached out his hand. "Jonathan Devons. Nice to meet you."

"Jim Hooper. I'm the local attorney-at-law here in Deadwood." He reached out and picked a piece of bark off Jonathan's shoulder. "Nice to meet you. I'd heard you were planning on leaving this week or next. Do you have a firm date yet?"

Jonathan shook his head, "No, but I'm sure everyone will know as soon as I leave."

Roberta felt like she was watching a tennis match with words replacing the ball. Words that were some sort of claim on her attention. She didn't like men fighting over her. Whoever she kept time with was and should be her decision. It was 1950 after all. She was of age to make her own decisions. "Nice to see you again, Mr. Hooper. Jonathan, are you ready to go? We have a full schedule tonight."

Jonathan beamed at her. He held out his arm, and she took it, despite the sawdust. "Good night, Mr. Hooper."

"Mr. Devons. I'm sure we'll run into each other again." Mr. Hooper tipped his hat to Roberta. "Good night, Miss Stevens. I expect my business will bring me back to the post office soon."

She nodded politely then started walking, dropping her hold on Jonathan's arm. Jonathan hurried to catch up with her.

"What was that about?" he asked.

"You tell me. You two looked like you were arguing over your favorite toy." Roberta turned to look at him.

"Sorry. I got a little possessive. He's a lawyer. From the rumors in town, he's looking to marry. I just thought—"

"You thought I was checking out my options? What is it with people out here? Everyone thinks I should be married or at least looking for a man to take care of me. Believe me, I'm not opposed to falling in love, but this time, it's going to be on *my* terms." They'd arrived at the general store. Roberta glanced at Jonathan's shirt and jeans, taking in the sawdust. "You stay out here, and I'll drop these off with Mr. Chase. Is noon tomorrow okay for lunch?"

He smiled at her. "It will be perfect."

She shook her head and headed into the store. They were busy, and Mr. Chase waved her to the counter on the back wall. She held up the pails and empty bottles. "Where do you want these?"

"You didn't have to return those. Jonathan could have brought them. He's working off his lunches with me right now." Mr. Chase chuckled as he took the pails from her and set them on a table. "I hear good things about your running of the post office. Most people say you're doing a much better job than I did."

She smiled at the compliment. "I'm enjoying the job. I'm trying not to get attached, but it's hard. There's a lot to learn and do, and I love that type of work. I just hope Mr. Smith gets here before I get too invested, or you might have to pull me out of the building, kicking and screaming."

"Have you thought about staying? I'm sure Mr. Smith could use your help. And if not him, I'm always looking for a little help. We'd keep you working—that's not a problem." Mr. Chase folded a blanket he'd taken out from under the counter.

"I'm actually thinking about it. I'm really enjoying the work. I feel like I have a purpose now."

Mr. Chase stopped folding. "Oh my dear, you've always had a purpose, and you're right where you need to be. Stop worrying. I'm sure everything will turn out for the best."

"Thank you. For the meals, for the job, and for believing in me. This stop was just what I needed at the time." She glanced back and saw Jonathan through the window. "I've got to go. I'll see you soon."

"You should come to the Methodist social Friday night. Everyone in town will be there. You'll meet a lot of your neighbors."

She smiled. "Actually, I plan on making a cake for it. Sarah Morris invited me."

"Sarah's such a good girl. She's lived in Deadwood all her life. Now she's raising her own children here." He waved toward the front, and Roberta saw that Jonathan was watching her.

"I've got to go. Lots to get done tonight." Roberta started moving to the exit through the crowded store.

"Have a good evening," Mr. Chase called after her. And then he chuckled again.

CHAPTER EIGHT

As they walked toward the boardinghouse, Roberta turned to Jonathan. "I feel like I should explain what I said just now."

"You mean about 'this time it would be on your terms'? I take it the last relationship didn't go so well?" He kept his voice low so they couldn't be overheard.

"Exactly." Roberta told him about meeting Philip and how their relationship had been on his terms and his timetable. "I knew it was going too fast, but I was enjoying the ride. He said he was head over heels in love with me and couldn't wait to start our new lives together, and I fell for it—hook, line, and sinker. I believed in him right up to the time he left me standing at the altar. All the cash money and gifts we'd been given before the wedding, his belongings—they were all gone the night before." She held up her right hand. "He asked for the ring back. Some story about getting it soldered with the wedding band. He said if he joined the rings together, no one could break us up. It sounded good, but something told me to hold on to it. Now it's my safety net. If this job doesn't turn out, at least I have this ring I can turn into some money."

"I didn't realize you had a recently ended relationship. I just figured you didn't have anything you wanted to do and that was how you showed up in Deadwood on a bus to Portland. I figured it was a lark." He took her hand. "I'm sorry he was such a jerk. I can't believe anyone would treat you like that."

"You broke off your engagement," Roberta reminded him. This wasn't about his last relationship, but the words came out a little harsh, even so.

"That was different." They were at the boardinghouse. "We can talk about this on our way. Give me ten minutes to clean up, and I'll be ready. Do you want to change? Or do you have time to talk to Mrs. Elliott about making us a basket?"

"I'll talk to Mrs. Elliott about our dinner." Roberta didn't have many outfits, and she already needed to do laundry on Saturday. "Besides, I have to deliver her mail."

By the time Jonathan returned to the kitchen, dinner had been packed and Roberta had handed over the mail, just like the manual described. She shook her head. It was going to be less exciting around here once the painting had been restored to its rightful owner and Mr. Smith took on his role as the town postmaster. Maybe less exciting wouldn't be that bad.

Jonathan opened the door to his sedan, and after he moved some maps and papers, she set the picnic basket in the back and got in the front. The car was nice inside. She'd never owned a car, because she'd lived close enough to work to not need one. This car could fit three or more kids in the back seat with no problem.

Not that she was judging Jonathan as a potential mate by his car. Or at all. Sarah had her confused with all her talk about finding a husband. When Jonathan got into the driver's side, she folded her hands and smiled at him.

"Do you like the car? Betsy was one of the first cars that came off the line in '46 when the auto industry started making vehicles again. I couldn't resist doing my part for the recovery effort." He grinned and tapped the car's dashboard.

"Seriously? That was your excuse to buy a new car?" She shook her head but couldn't stop the smile.

He shrugged. "I was a different man then. Very self-centered."

"I doubt that very much." She was determined to have a nice evening. No thinking about marriage or stolen paintings or leaving Deadwood. "So where are we off to?"

"I want to show you my favorite parts of the area." He started the car and backed up onto the street. "We'll go to the waterfall first, so we still have the light, then have a picnic in a meadow."

"Sounds lovely." She settled into the seat. This was so much more comfortable than her bus seat had been. Jonathan had driven to Deadwood in this while she sat in a huge box that liked to find every hole in the road. She watched the countryside. "I wish I had my drawing pad and pens. I would love to sketch at the waterfall."

"Did you leave them in St. Louis?" Jonathan glanced at her. He quickly returned his gaze to the road ahead.

"Actually, I'm hoping Mr. Smith has them. When he got off the bus, he took my travel case instead of his own."

Jonathan blinked then slowed down. "Did you look in his case?"

"Only to verify it was Mr. Smith's. Why?" Now she was curious.

"It's probably nothing. I'm just wondering what else he had in it. Maybe it has a clue as to why he's missing."

She shook her head. "I don't think so. But we can look in it when we get back. I'll bring it to the dining room, and you can search it for any secrets it might hold. But be warned, I will tell Mr. Smith that you went looking."

He nodded. "If he's on the up-and-up, he won't care. And it'll cross one more thing off our lists. What I've learned about investigating is that it's a lot of asking questions and finding out what's not true. That way you can scratch people off. Like you. You could be someone who charmed Mr. Smith out of his commission papers. Maybe you're looking for the painting too. You could want to return it to the people who stole it. People who now think that this Albert Gage is holding out on them. They want more of the money and sent you here to Deadwood to find the painting and turn it over to the rest of the gang."

"That's a wild story. So why did I call the FBI in on this when I had already bamboozled you and Mrs. Elliott? I could have taken the painting last night and left with my band of merry robber men." She could tell he was a writer. Making up what he didn't know came naturally, even when he was teasing her. At least she hoped he was teasing her.

"Maybe you're waiting for your ride out of town." He turned off the main road and onto a dirt one. It started getting bumpy immediately. "We'll go up to the fence line and park. Then it's a short walk to the falls. I should have told you."

"I have two pairs of shoes. The heels I wear to work and these. Unless we're walking in mud, I should be fine. Or I'll go barefoot." She wiggled her toes in the ballerina flats she wore most of the time. They were worn but comfortable. She didn't have the money to buy something new. Maybe after a few months of work she could put aside enough for a new pair. Depending on what her housing costs were in Portland. If she went to Portland. She was beginning to hope that, somehow, she could make a life here in Deadwood. She pushed aside the dream and focused on the road. The bumps were huge, and Jonathan had slowed the car's pace to try to minimize the damage. Both to the car and to the passengers.

"It is beautiful here." She rolled down the window and took in the scent of pine trees. There was a gentle breeze coming into the car, and it transported her from her worries about the future to just enjoying this moment. The present. She looked at Jonathan. "Do you know why it's called the present?"

He shook his head.

"Because each day is a gift from God. A present from Him." She leaned her head back and smiled, closing her eyes. "Thank you for bringing me out here. It's perfect. And a great memory of Deadwood."

"I was hoping it would be listed as a reason to stay, not just a cherished memory of the town after you leave."

She opened her eyes and looked at him. He was focused on the road ahead, not looking at her at all. And nothing in his face revealed his feelings. "It's not that simple. I love Deadwood. The people I've met have accepted me as one of their own. I've been invited to town events. And I enjoy my job. But I have to be realistic. If there isn't a job here for me, I'll have to leave."

As the car inched closer to their destination, she thought about Mr. Chase's offer to create a full-time job for her. One that would pay her living expenses. Could she trust him to fulfill his part of the bargain if she decided to stay?

Something inside of her laughed, and the sound was mean and cruel. Trust wasn't something she could give easily. Not after Philip.

"It sounds simple to me." Jonathan pulled the car over and parked in the grass in front of a barbed wire fence. "We'll have to walk from here."

What was he doing? He was trying to talk Roberta into staying in Deadwood when he was supposed to be leaving in the next few days. Or a week at most. Had he grown roots here? Was this where he wanted to build a life?

He got out of the car and pocketed the keys. After walking over to Roberta's side, he opened her door. He liked seeing her in his car. He decided, for just tonight, he'd take her advice. Live in the present. Live in the moment. He reached to help her out of the car. Her legs swung over the seat, and he was taken again with how beautiful she was. The best thing about her was she didn't even know it.

She saw him looking at her, and he felt his face flame. He turned his head and said, "I think your shoes should be sufficient."

As they walked the trail that was just wide enough for two, he talked about the reason he stopped in Deadwood in the first place. "I was tired of driving and not seeing the country. So when I got here, I asked Mr. Chase if there was a boardinghouse in town since, obviously, there weren't any motels. I think he must have seen something in me. Something that he wanted to nurture. To keep around Deadwood. Anyway, he sent me to Mrs. Elliott's and told me that before I left the next day I needed to visit the waterfall west of town. When I got here, I sat down with my journal and wrote for hours. I hadn't told Mrs. Elliott I was leaving yet, so when I went back to the boardinghouse, I paid for the week. I thought I'd be on the road as soon as the week was over, if not before. But I'm still here."

She looked up at him, wonder in her eyes. Had she already seen the life she could have here in this little town? Or was she thinking he was crazy? Because she was looking at him and not the trail, she stumbled over a tree root.

He grabbed her around the waist and pulled her up. They were face-to-face, and a sudden urge to kiss her made him lean closer.

Then she bit her lip.

He released her, knowing she was unsure of taking it to the next step. She smoothed her dress and, without looking at him, said, "Thank you. I thought I was going to fall. I don't have extra stockings, so that would have been a problem."

Jonathan looked at her. She wasn't going to even acknowledge what just almost happened. What kind of damage had her last fiancé caused to her heart? He wanted to say he wasn't that guy. That he wanted a future with her. But what could he offer right now? He worked at a lumber mill. He was estranged from his family. And he lived in one room at a boardinghouse. He needed roots before he decided to invite someone to share his life. He sure wasn't the eligible catch he'd been a year ago. Jonathan pointed down the trail. "We're almost there. Are you okay to keep going?"

"I only stumbled because I wasn't watching where I was going. I won't make that mistake again."

For a moment, Jonathan didn't know if she was talking about walking the trails, or their almost kiss. He hoped it was the former.

"Great, because you're going to love the view." He could be pleasant and distant. Or at least he hoped he could. He'd never felt this way about a woman before. This was new, and he wasn't sure he totally liked it. Especially how needy he felt to get a smile or a laugh from her.

He knew when she first spotted the waterfall through the trees, because she froze in place. He'd done the same thing that first visit. He came up behind her and put a hand on her arm. "There it is."

"It's magical. Now I really miss my pencils and sketchpad. My fingers are aching to try to capture this beauty, but I don't know that I'm good enough." She turned to him. "Can we get closer?"

"Of course. Take my hand so you don't slip in those shoes. The falls makes the trails damp."

"I can feel the drop in temperature around me." She grinned at him as they made their way down to the riverbank. "Does it have a name?"

"Wedding Veil Falls. According to stories, the first settlers in Deadwood used to hold their religious ceremonies here. Weddings, baptisms, even funerals. They didn't have a church, so this was the closest place they could feel God's power. At least that's the story Mrs. Elliott told me when I asked. Her husband asked her to marry him here. It's a popular place to pop the question."

She turned and looked at him strangely then moved over to a rock where she could sit and watch the water. "My first paycheck, I'm buying a drawing pad and pencils and hiring someone to bring me out here for a day. Then they can pick me up as the light leaves. I might just spend all my days off right here."

He smiled, hoping that her enthusiasm meant that maybe she was staying. "Mr. Chase would probably give you the pad and pencils now on credit for your first check. He already owes you for a couple of days."

She shook her head. "I'm not much for credit. I'd rather pay up front. That way I'm not beholden to anyone. And, once I know how much money I have, I can make smarter decisions on how much to spend. A girl's got to watch her budget, you know."

They sat there quietly for several minutes, just watching the waterfall. As they did, a doe and her fawn came to the riverbank and drank. Jonathan met Roberta's gaze, and she nodded. Neither one of them was willing to utter a word until the doe spotted them. She nudged her baby up toward the woods, and they bounded out of sight.

"That was the prettiest thing I've seen in years," Roberta whispered. "I mean, I knew there were deer here, but to see a mama and a baby? You've made my day. Maybe my month. Thank you."

"In all the time I've come here, I've never seen a doe or a fawn. I've seen badgers and otters swimming in the river. And fish jumping. But deer? You must be good luck." He stood and held out his hand to help her stand. "I hate to leave, but I've got one more place to show you, and we're losing daylight."

"Then let's get going. Although I'm not sure anything can top this." Roberta looked over her shoulder at the waterfall with tears in her eyes. "It makes your worries and thoughts kind of small to see something like this, doesn't it?"

By the time they made it back to the car, they were talking about where they'd gone to school and books they liked. Jonathan was happy to hear that Roberta was a reader as well as an artist. He offered to lend her his copy of Hemingway's latest book, only to find out she'd already read it. He had brought a box of books when he'd left home. He'd gone through most of them a second time and was now borrowing from the book collection the town had gathered for the new library.

"You should come to my room and go through my books sometime to see if there's anything you haven't read." He flushed as soon he said it. "Or I could bring the box to your room. Or the parlor."

"You're cute when you blush, did you know that?" Roberta teased. "I would like to see your collection, but I'd hate to borrow something then have to leave."

"I'm sure you'd do the right thing and leave the book with Mrs. Elliott. Or maybe even track me down to return it before you left." He rubbed his jawline as he drove the sedan back to the main road. "The next stop is just a few minutes away. What's your favorite book you read this last year?"

They talked about books, movies, and anything but the growing attraction between them. Jonathan noticed that, even when they disagreed, they both had logical arguments for their side. He could talk to her forever. As long as Monday never came.

CHAPTER NINE

Sitting in the meadow with Roberta was just the way he'd imagined it. The sun was over the mountains, starting to ease the day into night, as they finished their meal. She leaned back on the blanket, holding herself up by her arms, and watched the sunset.

"Mr. Devons, you know how to show a lady a nice time." She sighed as she looked over at him.

"My last girlfriend would disagree with that statement. Especially if I'd brought her here." He winced as he thought of Madeline. She would have hated walking to the waterfall and would rather eat in some fancy Chicago restaurant where they couldn't talk because of the noise but where she could be seen by the people who ran the town. "Sorry. I ruined the mood, didn't I?"

She shrugged. "We both have pasts. Why would I be upset if you talked about yours?"

She pulled her legs closer, and Jonathan realized the temperature was dropping.

"Are you ready to go?"

She nodded. "I'm a little chilled, and I still have work tomorrow. And a cake to bake for the Friday social. Would you care to be my date?"

He grinned as he returned everything to the basket then reached out his hands to help her up. "I don't know. How good are your cake-baking skills? Do I have to buy the cake just to make you look good and me gallant?"

"My cakes are passable. They taste good, but I'm not much of a decorator. Which is odd, since I have an artistic flair. I keep trying to fix things to make it perfect, but with frosting as a medium, you can't just erase the marks and try again. Well, you can, but then it gets messy. I promise that you won't be embarrassed by my cake if you accompany me."

"Well, it's a date then. Do you need help tomorrow baking?"

Her eyes widened. "Now you're a Renaissance man. Do you bake?"

He shook his head. "Not at all. But I could keep you company and maybe mix something if you need strong arms."

They were back in town when Constance waved them down. "Mama sent me to find you two. She says she needs to talk to you both, now. What did you do?"

"Nothing." Jonathan glanced over at Roberta.

She met his gaze. "Don't look at me. I didn't do anything."

"Get in. I'll drive you home," Jonathan said to Constance.

She looked across the street and stepped away from the car. "I'll walk home. Tell Mama I'll be there by nine."

Jonathan followed her gaze and saw a young man standing by the post office in the shadows. "Okay, then. I hope you're not getting me in trouble with your mother. You know I'm going to mention who you were with."

"She knows who I'm with. He was at the house when she asked me to come look for you." Constance smiled.

They drove away, a little faster now, toward the end of town where the boardinghouse was located. Jonathan grabbed the picnic basket out of the back seat then opened Roberta's door. "Let's go see what's going on."

Roberta followed him into the house, grateful for its warmth.

Dinner had been served, and the dining room was empty, so they went right to the kitchen.

Mrs. Elliott looked up, and relief showed on her face. "I'm so glad Constance found you."

"What's going on?" Jonathan set the picnic basket on the counter before moving over to the table where Mrs. Elliott sat, a letter in front of her.

She held up the letter. "This. I opened Bea's letter after dinner and found that Albert is planning on being here on the fifteenth."

"Saturday?" Roberta squeaked out the word. "But the FBI and the museum guys can't get here until Monday."

Mrs. Elliott looked up at her. "Who's coming?"

"I was going to tell you, but I got a little distracted." Roberta gave Jonathan a look, and he almost laughed. "Anyway, the museum people are coming to evaluate the paintings on Monday. If your nephew comes on Saturday to take them all, we might be in trouble for not stopping him."

"Well, the sheriff isn't going to be back in town until this weekend." Mrs. Elliott tapped a finger to her lips. "You and Jonathan are just going to have to take the paintings and hide them somewhere until Monday. Then maybe Albert will have left by the time the museum people get here, and we can get the paintings to the rightful owners. It's what Bea would have wanted."

"It will put you and Constance in danger," Jonathan said.

"I can handle myself. I'll send Constance to Portland on the Friday bus to see my sister, Hattie. She hasn't been there this year, and it will get her away from that boy. He's a little too close for my comfort right now."

Jonathan and Roberta shared a look.

"I know you think I'm being overprotective, but she's my only child." Mrs. Elliott sighed. "I'll put her on the bus, and then we can figure out where to stash the paintings."

"We could put them in the post office. No one knows that I've been looking at them. There are a lot of rooms that are just empty. Plenty of closets. We'll put them in an empty office Saturday morning." Roberta looked between Mrs. Elliott and Jonathan. "What do you think?"

Mrs. Elliott smiled. "We have a plan. Now I just have to call my sister and let her know to expect Constance."

After work on Thursday Roberta hurried to the boardinghouse to make her cake. Mrs. Elliott had offered to make one for her, but Roberta wanted to do this herself. Besides, Mrs. Elliott needed to get Constance ready for her trip to Portland. The girl had seemed flustered when her mom announced the visit at breakfast. Roberta figured it was because she and her boyfriend had made plans to meet up at the social on Friday night.

It was hard to be a teenager under your mother's watchful eye.

Jonathan was going directly to Bea's house to start getting the paintings packed and stored in the trunk of his car. Roberta would meet him there as soon as the cake was in the oven. Mrs. Elliott and Constance would decorate it if needed, but Roberta thought that she could carve out some time after dinner to finish it.

The workday had gone quickly. A lot of Deadwood residents had stopped by to see if they had mail, so she'd been kept busy. When she'd locked up the building, she wondered if this would be her last day as Deadwood's temporary postmistress. She was growing to love the town and the job and could even see a life for herself here.

All they had to do was keep several stolen paintings from being recovered by the thief who took them and wait for the FBI to take the paintings into their protection.

Just about a month ago, she was planning her wedding to the wrong guy. Now, she was hanging out with a man who could be Mr. Right. If the time was ever right. What would her new friends think of her if they found out that she'd recently been engaged? Would she be seen as pathetic or worse, especially after they found out that she'd been left at the altar?

She pushed her worries aside. They needed to keep Mrs. Elliott and Constance and the rest of the boardinghouse residents safe. That was her main concern now.

The flowers on the lilac bush were blooming as she walked up the sidewalk to the Elliotts' door, and she stopped for a second to take in the perfume. Yes, Deadwood was starting to feel like home. She'd miss it.

Roberta found Mrs. Elliott in the kitchen. She'd laid out on the counter all the ingredients and bowls and pans Roberta would need for the cake, along with the recipe.

She looked up from wrapping something on the table. "There you are. I hope your day at work wasn't too stressful."

Roberta went over and put on the apron that Mrs. Elliott had laid out. Then she went to wash her hands in the sink to get at least some of the ink off. "I think I've met every soul that lives in or around Deadwood by now. You've got a nice community here."

"Well, if there's anyone you haven't met, you'll see them tomorrow at the social. Someone from the post office in St. Louis called earlier. I took his number and put it on the dresser in your room. I didn't have the post office number, or I would have just given him that." Mrs. Elliott finished tying the string for the parcel. "Here's the hallway painting. I'll put it near the front door in the foyer so you can take it to Bea's when you go meet with Jonathan. Please thank him again for me. I don't know what I would have done without the two of you to help." She looked around the kitchen. "Now get busy on that cake. I need to check on Constance and her packing. She's taking everything she owns for a two-week trip."

"Is she okay with going?" Roberta picked up the recipe and scanned it.

Mrs. Elliott sighed. "Better than I am. I'm worried about her being on the bus for that long. I know she's got a good head on those shoulders, but I can't stop thinking about what could happen."

"She'll be just fine," Roberta said. "And I want to thank you for trusting us to help. I know we're strangers."

"Oh my dear, it's me who should be thanking you. You didn't have to get involved. This was my problem. You and Jonathan have been lifesavers."

Roberta turned the oven on then started measuring ingredients. It seemed foolish to be baking when an art thief was coming to town and they needed to protect the paintings, but on the other hand, she needed to pretend everything was normal. She hadn't participated in her high school's drama club, but now she wished she had learned how to act. It might be what kept them from being killed.

After the cake was in the oven, she set the timer and let Mrs. Elliott know she was walking over to Bea's house.

Roberta tucked the package under her arm and headed out the door, only to be stopped by Gerald, who'd just walked in the door.

"Good evening," she said to him.

"Good evening. Still thinking you'll get a job in Portland?"

"Yes, I am." She headed out the door, hoping he wouldn't ask any more questions.

Jonathan was outside Bea's house, putting things in the trunk, when she arrived. The house was separated from its closest neighbor by a hill and was on a dead-end street. So they shouldn't be seen loading up the paintings.

He took the package from her and placed it in the trunk as well, closing it after he did. "I think I got everything, but come walk through the house, just to make sure. My knowledge of art isn't as extensive as yours is, since you studied it in school."

"I'm sure you got everything, but I'll check. I don't remember everything I saw last time." She crossed over the lawn, which needed to be mowed, and entered the house.

Jonathan scanned the living room. "I don't see any art in here," he said as he went toward the kitchen.

"If Albert sent crystal or sculpture, she might have stashed it somewhere." Roberta checked the two cabinets in the living room. "There's nothing in here."

"Check the bedrooms. I'm stuck in the kitchen for a bit."

"Stuck? I can help," Roberta called back from the hallway.

He laughed. "Not that kind of stuck. There's just a lot of cabinets."

When they were done, they hadn't found anything else in the house. Roberta straightened a couch cushion and looked around. "I think if we hurry, we can still make dinner."

"Great, because I'm starving." He locked the door and handed Roberta the key. "Make sure you give this to Mrs. Elliott. She needs one to give to her nephew when he shows up. I sure hope she can keep her cool and play innocent when he asks her about the paintings."

"I'll give it to her as soon as we walk in the door or hang it on the key holder myself if she's busy." She moved to the passenger door and, without waiting for him to open it, she climbed in. When he got inside, she turned to him. "Are you too tired to help me decorate the cake after dinner?"

"Not at all." He started the car. "How was your day? I missed having lunch with you."

"It was good. Nothing exciting. Just a lot of people talking about the social. Sarah was right, there are a lot of people going."

He reached over and took her hand.

"What are you doing?"

"Sorry, it just felt right." He winked at her and let go of her hand. "Tomorrow night is a date, right? Or am I misunderstanding?"

"Sorry, it just took me by surprise." She watched out the window as they drove past the town square and her place of employment. At least for one more day. When Mr. Smith came to town, she'd be able to plan again.

She liked planning her life, almost as much as she loved drawing. But men were always changing her plans.

Well, that stopped now. From this day forward, she was going to set a plan and go for it. That way, she'd never worry about what she was going to be doing the next day, the next week, the next year. She'd have a plan.

She thought she heard someone laugh. What was the saying? *Man plans, God laughs.* At least she was providing God with plenty of humor these days.

CHAPTER TEN

Roberta checked her room one more time before going downstairs to breakfast. She'd gotten most of her clothes together besides the dress she planned on wearing tonight and the one she had on now. Mr. Smith's case sat on the bed as well. She'd take it with her to work. Then when the bus arrived at five thirty, she'd go welcome Mr. Smith to Deadwood and hand over his case. She hoped he'd give hers back as well.

She couldn't leave until Monday, when the paintings would be in the right hands. Well, actually, she *could* leave before that. Jonathan and Mrs. Elliott could take care of the transfer, but she wanted to be a part of it.

She touched the gold-plated *RS* on the brown leather. Of all the things to get her off her path to the new life in Portland, a mix-up of two cases and a man missing his bus hadn't seemed that consequential. Now those small things had changed her life. At least for a few days. Maybe she'd changed more than just what she wanted out of life. Maybe she'd found a home.

Roberta sat down at the breakfast table and took a plate of eggs and bacon from Mrs. Elliott. Constance sat across from Roberta. She was leaning her head against her hand and pushing her breakfast around with a fork with the other. "Constance, are you looking forward to your trip?"

The girl raised her gaze but not her head. "I guess."

"Constance is worried about her boyfriend forgetting her," Mrs. Elliott replied to Roberta.

"Mama," Constance whined.

Jonathan strode into the room. "If he really loves you, he'll be excited for you to take a vacation and see new things. He'll still be here when you return. Absence makes the heart grow fonder."

"Do you actually believe that?" Constance asked.

He nodded, sneaking a glance at Roberta. "He needs to appreciate having you around. And he can't do that if you're always around. If he's the one, he'll wait for you to come back from Portland, and he'll wait for you to decide what you want to do with your life before asking you to marry him. You both need time to be adults and find yourselves before making those choices."

"Nonsense. I met my wife right out of high school, and the next year we had babies to feed. There wasn't any running around 'finding' ourselves. We were never lost." Gerald reached for another biscuit.

"That was ages ago, Gerald. I certainly hope you aren't advising my daughter to get married to the first man who asks. What about love?" Mrs. Elliott passed Gerald the butter.

"Love will come," he said. "She'll figure it out. She seems to be a smart girl."

Roberta turned to Constance. "Finding the one you want to spend the rest of your life with is all well and good. But weren't you talking about going to school and working a few years before starting a family? Your goals and dreams are important too."

"But then I'll be as old as you are." Constance's eyes went wide and she covered her mouth with her hand.

"Constance, that was rude." Mrs. Elliott glanced over at Roberta. "Tell Miss Stevens you're sorry."

"I'm sorry, that came out wrong." Constance blushed. "Mama, may I be excused? I'm not very hungry."

"Of course, dear." Mrs. Elliott watched as her daughter carried her plate to the kitchen. "She's upset."

"It's fine. I didn't take offense. I've been called an old maid before." Roberta took the last bite of her eggs. "But right now I need to get to work. According to the manual, Fridays are busy in a post office. People want to buy money orders." Roberta took her plate and glass into the kitchen, and Jonathan followed her.

"I'll see you tonight at the social. I need to collect my paycheck before I leave the lumber mill, and they're often a little late passing them out." He set his plate in the sink next to hers. "Are you ready for tomorrow morning? We'll need to get to the post office early. Before breakfast. We don't want to be sitting at the table when Albert arrives."

"I'm ready. Maybe we should skip the social and store the paintings tonight." She took a deep breath. "I feel like someone in a spy novel. Jumping into a situation without knowing what's going to happen. I sure hope Mr. Carver and his FBI friend show up on Monday like they're supposed to."

He squeezed her shoulders. "Don't worry. I have a plan."

"I like having my own plans, thank you." She turned and leaned against the counter. "Maybe I won't like your plan."

"Maybe not, but it's the one we've got. And we're not skipping the social. See you tonight." He waved and headed out the door.

"So much for walking me to work or whispering sweet nothings in my ear." She turned to go back to the dining room because she'd left her case—Mr. Smith's case—under the table.

"Who are you talking to, dear?" Mrs. Elliott had come into the kitchen and stood near the door.

"Jonathan, but he just left." Roberta hurried out of the kitchen before Mrs. Elliot could ask more questions or see the heat in her cheeks. She picked up the case, and after checking her hair in the mirror by the door, she stepped out onto the front porch and into what could very well be her last day of work in Deadwood.

The post office was as busy as the manual had suggested the day would be. She didn't have time to go get her lunch, so Mr. Chase sent it with a customer who was looking for mail. When she had a break from customers, she went to sort the last of the mail Jonathan had dropped off yesterday from Mr. Chase.

A parcel had come for Jonathan Devons. It felt like a book, but the handwriting was scrolled and flowery. She set it by her purse to remember to give it to him tonight. Her thoughts went to the parcel several times that day. She was tempted to open it, but as the manual said, opening another person's mail wasn't allowed. In fact, it was a crime.

She didn't want to commit a crime or pry into Jonathan's life. With them hiding the paintings, it felt like they were already involved in a crime. One she didn't want to be part of, but she couldn't risk those paintings disappearing just because she couldn't be brave.

She squared her shoulders and went back to work.

Finally, it was time to close the post office. She did all the closing tasks and put Jonathan's package into her purse. Then she took out the key and locked the building. She hoped this wouldn't be the last time she locked this door. But if it was, she had worked hard, and the Deadwood post office was ready to become part of the community. Mr. Smith would love it here, and his father would be proud of him and how the younger Smith carried his name.

The bus passed her on the street, so by the time she got to the general store, Mrs. Elliott was already getting Constance settled on the bus. The driver waved at her, and she went over to talk to him.

"How are you getting along? Ready to head to the big city?" He grinned at her.

Roberta shook her head. "Actually, I still have a few things to clean up here. Did Mr. Smith arrive?"

"You mean the man who disappeared from my bus? Actually, no. But he did send you a case and a letter." The driver reached back and handed her a tan case that matched the one in her hands. She took it and the letter and went to sit on the bench outside the general store.

Dear Miss Stevens,

I'm sorry I grabbed the wrong case when I left the bus last week. I suspect you're missing your pens and paper much more than I am the postal commission. I admit I was scared of taking the job. Scared of leaving the woman I love. So I hid until the bus left then got a ride back to St. Louis on the next one. I called the post office and let them know I'm not taking the position. They told me that you've been working there while the town waits for my arrival. Please send my case to me at the following address, cash on delivery. If you're interested in a job, they're looking for a postmaster/mistress in Deadwood.

Best wishes,
Bob Smith

Roberta was floored. Mr. Smith wasn't coming to take her job. She wondered if that was why she'd gotten the call from the St. Louis post office. With everything that had been going on with the paintings, the message Mrs. Elliott had given her had slipped her mind.

The driver picked up a clipboard and walked toward her. "I'm coming back through Deadwood next Friday if you want to continue your journey then."

She thanked him and went to stand with Mrs. Elliott, who was outside Constance's window, watching her daughter. She took her landlady's arm. "You're keeping her safe."

"I know." Mrs. Elliott wiped a tear from her cheek. "I just hope I'm not sending her from the frying pan into the fire."

"She'll come home with all kinds of new stories and ideas. It's good for young women to travel a bit. And she has her aunt and her family." Roberta hugged Mrs. Elliott. "You're a good mother."

The bus started up, and they waved to Constance, who was grinning like it was Christmas. As the women walked back to the house, Roberta said to Mrs. Elliott, "She won't be smiling after sitting an hour in those hard red seats. She'll come home grateful for her bed and her life."

Mrs. Elliott laughed. "You're not supposed to make me feel better. I'm supposed to be a mess right now."

Roberta hooked elbows with her new friend. Things were working out.

Jonathan glanced around the lumber mill. Roland Farmer still hadn't come out with the checks. He looked at his watch again. "The bank is going to be closed by the time they pay us."

Frank eyed him. "What's up with you? You got some big plans with that pretty girl?"

"No." Jonathan's denial came out too strong.

Frank chuckled. "I knew it. You're taking our new postmistress to the social over at the Methodist church tonight. Is she baking a cake for you to buy?"

"I think it's a cake walk. You walk in a circle, and if you're the last person standing, you get to pick a cake. I'm not sure what cake Roberta is making." He stood and stretched. "How long does it take to write a few checks?"

"I don't understand all that business stuff. I just do my job, and on Fridays, I get my money. It's a fair trade." He rolled his shoulders. "I too am attending the Methodist social. That girl from the store, Amanda? She asked if I'd accompany her. I guess you turned her down?" Frank stared at him.

"I didn't turn her down. Well, maybe I did. But I didn't know Roberta and I were going to be going. I'm gonna look like I was waiting for someone better to ask me, at least in her eyes. I hate it if I hurt her." Jonathan sank onto a stack of boards. "I wasn't planning on staying here. You know that."

"I'll tell her. But I will also tell her that sometimes love can't be predicted or controlled. You're in love with this Roberta? The girl from the post office?"

"It's been less than a week. How could I be in love with her?" Jonathan's hands were sweating.

"I didn't ask you how long you've known her." Frank smiled and slapped Jonathan on the back. "Are you in love with Roberta? It's a simple question. Yes or no?"

Roland burst out of the office with envelopes in his hand. "Paychecks are ready."

"Got to go." Jonathan didn't wait to hear Frank's response, but he did hear his laughter following him. Did he love Roberta? He reached for the envelope Roland held out to him. "Thanks."

"Don't thank me, you did the work. I'll see you next week?"

"That's my plan. I'll see you Monday."

"I hope so, boy. You're good people, and we could use more of those around here." Roland glanced at the next envelope and called out a name.

Jonathan sprinted out of the lumber mill and right to the bank. The door was still open. He rushed to a cage. "I didn't think I'd make it."

"We heard they were running late paying at the mill, so we stayed open for you guys." The woman took his check and turned it over. "You need to sign this. Do you want me to put it all into your account? Or do you need some cash?"

"Actually, this time, give me some cash." He quickly estimated what might be needed for the weekend. If Albert showed up, he and Roberta might take a drive in the country for the day. That way she'd be out of danger. He hoped the FBI would be here on Monday like they said. He'd love to take her to the ocean, but they weren't at that stage of their relationship.

"Mr. Devons? Mr. Devons?"

Jonathan realized he'd been lost in thought. "Sorry, what did you ask me?"

"How do you want your money? Anything special?"

After he left the bank, he went to the boardinghouse. He ate a sandwich in the kitchen with Mrs. Elliott as she told him her concerns about having Constance in Portland. Then he went out to the sedan and checked that it was locked up. He pocketed the keys. He'd be ready to move the paintings first thing in the morning. Hours before Albert Gage arrived with any of his gang. Roberta had mentioned doing it tonight, but there was no way he was missing his date with her.

Glancing at his watch, he realized the social was about to start, so he moved to the sidewalk.

"I didn't take you for a religious man." A voice came from out of the dark.

Jonathan squinted, and his gaze landed on Gerald sitting in a rocking chair. "Excuse me?"

"I take it you're heading to that social with the Methodists. I just didn't see you as the religious type." Gerald stood and leaned against a porch column.

"They have cake. I'm a big fan of cake. Are you coming? We could walk together. Talk about current events."

"No, I'll stay here. Maybe Mrs. Elliott will bring one home and we'll have cake with dinner tomorrow. Just keep your head on your shoulders. I assume you're going with that Miss Stevens. Are you two a couple now?"

Jonathan froze. Gerald was the second person today to comment on Jonathan's feelings for Roberta. Was he that transparent? And how did they know he was in love when he didn't know himself? He shook off the question and waved at the older man. He didn't have time for second-guessing himself. He and Roberta were on a quest to save those paintings. Now he just hoped they could do it.

When he reached the church, the event was already in progress. He moved past the women who were selling tickets to the cake walk and entered the large hall. It was where they also held services, so the pews had been moved to the sides, and the altar and pulpit were up on the stage. He could just see them through the slit in the curtains that had been pulled across the front. It looked like his school gym back in Chicago. He'd gone to a private school, so the large gym had served a lot of purposes. Just like this building in Deadwood.

He scanned the room for Roberta, and his breath caught when he spotted her talking to Mr. Chase. He moved over to where they stood, and she smiled at him as he approached. "Good evening," he said. "I hope I'm not late."

She took his arm. "Mr. Chase was nice enough to keep me company. He just gave me the news that I'll be running the post office for another week or so. Or at least until they find a replacement."

"Mr. Smith didn't arrive on the bus, I take it." He tore his gaze away from Roberta and shook Mr. Chase's hand.

"No, and from the call I got from my contact at the post office, he's not taking the position. Miss Stevens showed me a letter he sent her which confirms it. I put in a good word for our current postmistress, and they'll call me on Monday to give me an update." Mr. Chase saw someone across the room. "Sorry, I'm being hailed. I'll take my leave now that your date is here."

Roberta waited a minute then tugged him across the room. "Mr. Chase told you part of my news, but I've got something for you," she said, moving ahead of him.

"Not another painting." Jonathan hurried to catch up. They found an empty hallway that led to an office. "Don't we have enough art to save?"

"It's not a painting." She pulled a wrapped parcel out of her bag. "This came for you. I'm just doing my job. Delivering the mail."

"You look too pretty in that dress to be working," he said, but he took the package anyway. He glanced at the return address and grinned. Ripping off the paper, he uncovered a brown journal. His name was embossed in the bottom right corner. Or at least his old name. His mother had sent the journal to tell him she loved him, no matter what. He showed it to Roberta. "It's a gift from my mother."

She reached out to touch the leather cover, but he hid the name with his hand before she got close enough to read it.

"It's really nice. I looked at one like it for my drawings, but it was a little pricey for my budget."

He shoved the journal into his suit pocket. "Thank you for bringing this to me. It means a lot."

"Well, now you have something to do while we hang out this weekend. Write." Roberta held her finger to her lips, listening. "Sounds like the cake walk is starting. Maybe I should show you my cake so you don't accidentally choose it."

He smiled at her. "Apparently, that's the point of this whole event. I'm supposed to choose your cake." *And you*, he added silently, watching her twist a strand of her red hair as they walked back to the gathering.

CHAPTER ELEVEN

Before the music started, Mr. Chase pulled Jonathan and Roberta off the floor and back to the same hallway they'd just come from. "Mrs. Elliott sent me. You need to move the paintings as soon as possible. Her nephew, Albert Gage, just walked in the door."

Jonathan stepped to where he could see the front door. "The man in the black suit and fedora she's talking to. That's Albert Gage?"

"Yes, and he looks just as mean as he did when he lived here. She said you need to go now. Don't worry. I'll watch out for her." When they didn't move, he took ahold of their arms and hurried them to a back door. "She told me what you two were doing, so you need to get those paintings moved. I'm not sure having them in a car will protect them if it should happen to rain tonight or this weekend."

He pushed them outside and shut the door.

Jonathan took her hand and started walking to the boardinghouse and his car. "I should have moved the paintings tonight, but I really thought we had more time."

Roberta walked quicker to match his pace. "He's not expecting us to know anything, so it'll be okay."

Just to be safe, before they arrived at the boardinghouse, Jonathan stopped at the town square. "Sit here and wait for me, just in case Albert sent someone to the house. I'll go get the car and come get you."

"Okay."

He turned back and saw the fear on her face. He squeezed her hand. "You'll be safe. If you feel uncomfortable out in the open, go to the post office and lock yourself inside. You have your key, right?"

When she nodded, he left her at what he now considered their bench.

Jonathan didn't want to leave her alone, but on the other hand, he didn't want to be surprised by some of Gage's friends hanging out at the boardinghouse.

As he'd feared, there were three men on the porch, talking to Gerald.

Gerald must have seen Jonathan quietly approaching, because he stood up. "I don't know about you boys, but I could use some coffee. Let's go in and see what Mrs. Elliott has in the kitchen. I'm sure she wouldn't want her nephew's friends left on the porch."

One of the men stood up from where he'd been leaning on the porch rail. "I could use some coffee."

Another man scanned the empty street. "Nothing in this one-horse town to watch anyway," he said as he followed the other men into the house.

Three men plus Gage. And the sheriff was an hour away. This was not good. Jonathan hurried to the car, unlocked it, and slipped inside.

As he drove away, he watched the house in his rearview mirror. One of Gage's men came out on the porch and watched him. Then Gerald came back out and handed the guy a cup of coffee. He pointed to the car and then to the house next door.

He hoped Gerald had sold the story, but Jonathan didn't hang around to check. All he needed to do was get the paintings into the post office. He drove down Main Street to the town square where he'd left Roberta.

She wasn't there.

He parked the car behind the post office. After he got out and locked the door, he looked around. From where he stood, he could see all the benches in the dim light, and not one was occupied. She must have gone into the post office.

Light shone from the windows. He went to the deliveries door and knocked. "Roberta, it's me, Jonathan. Let me in."

No response.

"Roberta, let me in." He raised his voice.

Glancing back at the car, he hoped it was hidden enough or that they wouldn't recognize it from being parked at the boardinghouse. Did he have time to move all the paintings into the post office for safekeeping?

The door flew open, a hand squeezed his shoulder, and Jonathan found himself being pulled inside the post office. "What's going on?"

"Be quiet. They're out front, but I don't think they know what they're looking for. They just followed you here. Why didn't you take off out of town?" The man rattled off questions, and Jonathan blinked in the dim light.

"Who are you, exactly?"

"Edwin Martin. I'm with the FBI. Now where are those paintings? If Albert Gage finds you, he won't let you live long enough to testify against him."

Jonathan looked around and saw Roberta with a man standing beside her.

She pointed to Martin. "He said he's with the FBI." She indicated the man next to her. "This is John Carver from the museum. They found me on the bench, and we came here to talk."

Jonathan sank onto a stool. "Why is everyone early this week? Not that I'm complaining, exactly, but you weren't supposed to be here until Monday."

"Once Mr. Carver here told me what Miss Stevens had told him, we researched Albert Gage. I knew he'd be here sooner or later to reclaim his property. Especially when he found out his mother had passed away. You should have moved quicker. Now, where are the paintings? We need to get them out of here." Martin glanced out the window. "You did a good job parking your car behind the post office. It looks like it's hidden from the front and could be mistaken for a rural route vehicle. Maybe we should take that when we leave."

"Thanks, I think." Jonathan glanced at Roberta. She looked nervous and was chewing her bottom lip. "I think Roberta and I should leave now. You seem to have everything in order."

"It's too late for that. You two just need to stay here in the post office. I've got backup coming." Martin pointed to a doorway. "What's in there?"

"The sorting room," Roberta replied.

"No windows or doors to the outside?"

She shook her head. "No. It's surrounded by offices, the front counter, and this delivery area."

Martin pointed toward the door. "You three go in there and sit down. I'll be back in a few minutes."

They hurried into the room and shut the door. Then Roberta turned on a desk lamp to ease the darkness. She moved it closer to John Carver. "Something's wrong. What is it?" she asked.

Carver glanced at the door. "I don't know what you mean."

"He's wearing dirty shoes and doesn't have a badge. He looks a lot like the man on a wanted poster out on my lobby wall." Roberta stared at the man. "Are you going to tell us what's going on?"

"I don't think Martin is actually FBI. He's not my normal contact. He met me at the airport in Portland when I arrived from New York. My secretary told me that someone had called and asked her a ton of questions about your call and my upcoming trip. When I got off the plane he said that Nathan, my regular contact, sent him. When I asked to see his badge, he said he'd left it at home."

Jonathan groaned. "And I just brought him all the paintings."

"You didn't say anything about the paintings being in the car. I told him we'd taken them to someone's country house a few days ago." Roberta sat down and wrung her hands. "I was scared you were going to tell him, but you didn't. I don't think we'd be alive right now if you had. I think he's holding us as collateral."

"So the real guys are coming on Monday?" Jonathan looked over at Carver. "When they find you gone, will they come looking?"

Carver shrugged. "I don't know. I hope Nathan came looking for me when I didn't show up at the Portland office. If so, he should be here anytime."

"Okay, then we just have to stay alive until he shows up or the sheriff gets back from his vacation. Easy peasy." Jonathan glanced over at Roberta. "Do you want to try to get to the car? If he's out front, talking to his guys, it's probably now or never."

Roberta took a breath. She wasn't the adventuresome type, no matter what her actions in the last week would lead anyone to believe. Jonathan was right. If they were to keep the thieves from the art and, more importantly, stay alive, they needed to act. Now. She looked over at Carver, who looked pale, even taking into consideration the dim lighting. "Mr. Carver, are you with us?"

"If they catch us leaving, they might kill us." He ran a hand through his hair, clearly frustrated with the choice. "But, on the other hand, if we stay here—"

"Staying here isn't an option." Jonathan turned to Roberta. "Just two doors to this room?"

"Yes. The one we came in goes to the loading dock area, and that one"—she pointed—"goes to the customer lobby area."

Roberta watched as Jonathan went over to the door she'd just pointed out. *Please let no one be watching*, she prayed. He opened the door a crack then shut it again.

"They're standing out in the lobby by the door. Albert Gage is with them, and so are the three other men who were at the house." Jonathan walked back to where they were. He nodded to the table. "Carver, help me block the door with this so it'll slow them down. Roberta, get to the other door, and be ready to run."

Roberta moved to the door. After the men positioned the table, they joined her. Jonathan took the keys to the car out of his pocket.

"Run to the car. I'll unlock the driver's door, and you two be ready to get into the back seat. Stay down."

Roberta reached over and squeezed his hand. "Be careful," she whispered.

He met her gaze. "You too."

"Are we ready?" Carver asked.

"Yes."

Carver opened the door a crack, and when he didn't see anything, opened it wider and slipped through, running to the loading dock door. He waved for the others to follow.

Jonathan gently pushed Roberta out into the area, and then she felt his arm around her waist as he joined her and they ran to the door Carver held open. He shut it behind them and followed them to the car.

Jonathan unlocked the front door then reached in to unlock the back door. Carver opened it, and Roberta dove in first. She curled up on the floor on the far side as Carver jumped in after her and closed the door.

Jonathan started the engine. He'd just put the car in gear when lights flashed and someone spoke through a megaphone. "This is the police. Get out of the car."

Carver kicked open the door and fell out of the car. Jonathan immediately shut off the engine.

Roberta slowly got off the floor and climbed out of the car. She couldn't see anything with the lights in her eyes, but all of a sudden, someone took her arm and led her toward the row of lights.

"Are you all right, miss?" the uniformed officer asked her as they made their way to where several men were huddled around a truck. There were four or five men on the ground with their hands tied behind their backs. She recognized one as the guy who called himself Edwin Martin. It might have been his real name, but he wasn't an FBI agent. He was just another crook.

Jonathan stood with the men by the truck, and she ran to him. "What's going on?"

He grinned and looked around "This is the real FBI and Sheriff Flagstaff. I guess he cut his vacation short when the FBI agent called him yesterday."

She leaned against him, not caring what people thought. She wasn't sure she could stand on her own. "Is it over?"

"Yes. I gave them my keys, and they're unloading the stolen paintings from my car now. We should be able to get back to our normal lives tomorrow."

"Don't forget you'll have to testify in their trials when they come up, unless someone confesses." The FBI agent raised his voice. "We'll have a nice little deal for that guy." When none of the men on the ground said anything, he shrugged. "It was worth a try."

The next morning, Roberta came downstairs in a dress Mrs. Elliott had loaned her last night when they returned from the post office. All Roberta's clothes needed to be washed. She went into the dining room. She was starving. She'd been too scared to eat dinner last night. Everyone was at the table already. Well, besides herself and Constance, who was in Portland. She poured herself a cup of coffee from the credenza and settled next to Jonathan. "Good morning. I guess I was tired."

"Helping to arrest a group of art thieves can do that to a person." Gerald smiled at her. "I hear you were quite resourceful. For a woman."

Roberta took the plate of pancakes Mrs. Elliott held out to her. "Thanks, Gerald."

Jonathan caught her eye. "Do you want to go for a drive after breakfast? I have something I want to show you."

She paused before taking the bite of pancakes dripping with syrup. "I'd love to."

An hour later, when they got to the pasture where they'd had their picnic a few nights before, she frowned. "You showed me this meadow already. It's really pretty."

He shut off the engine. "I want to show you something else."

She met him at the front of the car. "Okay, what's going on?"

"Do you see that fork in the road up on the mountain there?" He pointed to the left.

"Yes."

He pointed to the right. "See the barn and pasture?"

"Barely, why?"

"And the river over past this meadow?"

"Yes, I see it. Jonathan, what are we doing out here?" Roberta turned and looked at him.

He went down on one knee and took her hand. "I don't have a ring yet. This all happened quickly, but after last night, I need to ask you a question."

Roberta's blood was pumping in her ears. Her legs quivered, and her mouth felt dry.

"I bought this land yesterday. I believe a house would go perfectly over there by the trees, if you agree."

She nodded. "It's almost picture perfect."

He squeezed her hand again. "It will be. As long as you agree to share it with me. I know we just met, so it doesn't have to be tomorrow, but it has to be soon. I want to start my new life. And I want you by my side. I love you, Roberta Stevens. Will you marry me?"

She felt the tears but didn't know why she was crying. She swallowed the lump in her throat. "Yes, Jonathan Devons. I will marry you."

"About that name. I need to tell you something." He stood and leaned against the car as he told her about his history and his family. "I just want you to know exactly who you're marrying. There can't be any lies between us, even ones of omission."

She kissed him. "I love you, no matter what your past or your name is."

On the drive back to Deadwood, she saw a package on the floor. Picking it up, she looked over at Jonathan. "Did the agents forget one of the paintings?"

"That's not a painting. Open it up." He grinned at her.

She opened the packet, and a drawing pad and a box of pencils dropped into her lap. "Oh my, these are lovely. Are they for me?"

"I bought them so you'd have something to do while we waited for the FBI, but they decided to show up early, so I didn't have time to give them to you."

"I love them." She spent a few moments thinking of the first drawing she was going to make as soon as they got back to the boardinghouse. A house in a meadow by a barn with trees and a river behind it. She could see it in her mind's eye. Their home.

As they drove into town, she imagined her future, sketching the house, with a sky so blue it made her eyes hurt. And on the blanket next to her, her baby girl, whose eyes were the same color of blue, watching her.

"You're awfully quiet over there. Are you sure you're okay with this? With us? Do you want to stay in Deadwood, or go back to St. Louis? Or Portland?" He peppered her with questions as he drove.

She leaned closer and laid her hand on his arm. "I'm perfect. When I moved to Oregon, I learned that it's not who you've been, it's who you become in life. The good thing about Deadwood is, it's a great place to be reborn."

THE HEART OF THE MATTER

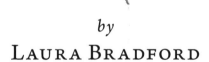

by

LAURA BRADFORD

"Have faith in God," Jesus answered.

—MARK 11:22 (NIV)

◈ CHAPTER ONE ◈

Deadwood, Oregon
Present Day

Penny McCormick looked from the run-down house to the framed painting in her hands and back again, her whole body sagging in defeat. If she didn't know any better, she'd think she'd made a wrong turn or that she was in the midst of yet another nightmare. But she *did* know better, and the number of pinches she'd given herself just in case only served as unwanted confirmation.

It was official. The home her grandparents, Jonathan and Roberta Devons, had built together to house their love story some seventy years earlier bore little resemblance to the painting that had hung in Penny's childhood home for as long as she could remember. She knew, on some level, it shouldn't be a surprise considering it had been vacant for close to thirty years now. But somehow, the stories she'd grown up hearing from her mother had frozen this place in Penny's imagination as if the laughter, joy, and the picture-perfect life inside its four walls were still happening, in real time.

Leaning against the car behind her, she traced her index finger along the outline of what the place in front of her had once been— the inviting front porch, the window boxes with their colorful flowers, the porch swing, the pitcher of lemonade resting on a table beside a pair of rocking chairs… It had been so perfect, so welcoming, so warm. And now—

Penny lifted her gaze to the current state of the painting's subject and blinked against the very tears she'd been trying to run from. It wasn't that she'd thought a place—particularly one she'd never been to—could ease the unrelenting pain of her mom's passing. But she'd certainly hoped that coming here, to the place where her mother had been raised and the grandparents she'd never known had once lived, would have made her feel less alone. Less like someone who, at the age of twenty-five, literally had no living family members left.

Yet here she was, in Deadwood, Oregon, of all places, standing in front of a dilapidated version of her mother's prized possession. And what did she have to show for it? Absolutely nothing. Except the nearly 2,500 miles she'd put on her already too-high odometer.

"Brilliant move, Pennykins," she murmured. "Brilliant move."

For a moment, maybe two, she gave some real thought to getting back into the car and round-tripping it straight back to Knoxville, Tennessee, but as fast as the thought came, she pushed it away. Her mother had left her this place because she'd wanted Penny to see it. To experience it. To feel it. And, most importantly, to feel *them* inside it.

It was a sentiment her head had resisted in the immediate aftermath of her mother's death, but when all of the well-wishers who'd filled the funeral home had returned to their lives, coming here to this place had been the lifeline she'd desperately needed to keep from drowning.

But now?

Blowing out a breath, Penny set the painting on the hood of her car and made herself move in the direction of the house. The years and years of neglect were evident everywhere she looked.

The stone walkway her grandfather had laid by hand was nearly impossible to find amid the potpourri of waist-high grass, wildflowers, and weeds that swayed in the not-so-gentle October breeze.

The porch that had looked so inviting in acrylic, looked old and tired in reality, as if Mother Nature could blow it off the house at any moment. The porch swing she'd always imagined sitting on was rotting in places. The pair of rocking chairs had fared no better than the swing, and the table between them was nowhere to be seen.

The flower box on the left-side window clung to the house's exterior by only one nail, and the one on the right had obviously played host to many a wasp nest over the years.

With slow, tentative movements, she picked her way through the vegetation to the front steps. They creaked and groaned under the weight as they delivered her to the door. She drew in a long breath, held it to a silent ten-count, and then slipped the key into the lock. When it clicked yet didn't give, she added a little shoulder power and a determined, if not wary, shove to the mix until she was staring into a hallway and its hundreds of dust motes dancing in the stale, sun-filled space.

She peeked around the open door and heard the echo of her gasp. To the left, just as her mother had described in stories, was the coatrack Penny's grandfather had made by hand for her grandmother. And, sure enough, at the very top of the handcrafted piece, was the small bear whittled from the wood of a tree taken down to make room for the house.

Running her fingers along the rack's wooden arms, Penny marveled at the craftsmanship and smiled at the one positioned low enough on the pole so as to be accessible to the child-sized version of her mother. And, just like that, the tears that had been so quick to flow in the weeks leading up to and following her mother's passing made their way down her cheeks.

This house had been where her grandparents, Grandpa Jon and Grandma Roberta, had begun their life as a married couple. They'd had joys and sorrows, milestones to celebrate and lost opportunities to mourn, and everything else life could throw at them in the place where Penny now stood. And her mother had entered the world in this very home—a place she'd looked back on fondly and talked about often throughout her too-short life.

Step by step, Penny moved into the hallway, her curiosity to see overshadowing any apprehension stirred up by the home's outward appearance. Sure, thick dust coated everything. Sure, there was a musty, closed-up smell that permeated the air and made it difficult to breathe. But there was also a sense of familiarity that was so strong, she couldn't do anything but keep going, keep looking, keep imagining.

The kitchen with its hand-carved table she'd seen in the background of more than a few birthday party pictures…

The den with its fireplace that had once roared with life on cold, winter mornings…

The funny creak in the second stair from the bottom that her mother had to be mindful of while indulging in a late-night snack in her teen years…

The hand-stitched comforter that still covered the bed her grandparents had shared…

The window seat in the smaller of the two bedrooms that had been her mother's favorite reading spot…

It was all there. Just as she'd been told. And while the years hadn't been kind in many aspects, Penny could, indeed, feel them all there with her, especially her mom.

Suddenly, it didn't matter how overgrown the yard was or how much work it was going to take to return the house to its original luster. No, the only thing that mattered was being there. In a place they'd once been all together, enjoying life and loving one another.

Her mind made up, Penny pulled a notebook and pen from her shoulder bag, turned to the first empty page she could find, and began a list of the many, many things that needed to be done over the next three weeks.

CHAPTER TWO

The strand of bells above the glass door jingled as Penny stepped inside the local hardware store she'd spied on her way into town earlier in the day. It wasn't the big-box store she was used to in Tennessee, but it was worth a shot. If nothing else, she was confident they'd have some of the more basic items on her list.

"Welcome to Foster's." A woman Penny guessed to be in her late fifties or early sixties stepped out from behind a nearby counter with a welcoming smile and a name tag bearing the name RITA. "May I point you to what you need?"

Penny returned the smile as she lifted her notepad and gave it a little shake. "Yes, please. Though, fair warning, you might need more than the average allotment of fingers for all this."

"That's why I wear sandals to work most days—gives me ten more options."

It felt strange to laugh and even stranger to hear herself doing it. "Ah, a wise woman indeed."

"May I see your list?"

She handed the notepad to Rita. "If you don't have all of it, I understand. But whatever you *do* have will at least get me started."

"Let's take a look, shall we?" Rita made her way down the list, bobbing her head at every line. When she reached the end, she flashed Penny a thumbs-up. "You're in luck. We've got it all. I'll just need to get some of the bigger items from the garage."

Penny looked from Rita to the notepad. "You have all of this?"

"We do."

"Outstanding!"

"Is your truck parked in the lot on the side or out front on the street?" Rita asked, skimming her way down the list once again.

Penny opened her mouth to answer, only to close it and swallow. Hard.

Rita's gaze lifted to Penny, traveled across her shoulder to the parking lot visible from the store's side windows, and, after the briefest of moments, landed back on Penny. "Did you walk?"

"No. I drove. I parked on the street out front. But my car isn't much bigger than a breadbox." She rocked on the heels of her ankle boots and let loose a frustrated sigh. "I didn't think this through too well, I see."

Rita waved away Penny's words before they were even fully clear of her lips. "No worries, dear. I can have all of your bigger items on the list delivered to you after five o'clock."

"You can do that?" Penny asked.

"Of course."

"*Phew.* That's a relief." Penny followed Rita to the counter and a computer monitor housed on a tabletop to the left of the register. "What's your delivery charge?"

Rita set the notepad next to the monitor. "Assuming it's within twenty miles, there's no charge."

Penny wandered her thoughts down the rural roads she'd taken to get there and shrugged. "I'm not sure. I didn't think to notice that on the way over here."

"What's your address, young lady?" Rita asked, readying her fingers on the keyboard. "I can look it up."

"Oh, sure. It's 15 Sunrise Knoll."

Rita drew back and stared at Penny. "Did you say Sunrise Knoll?"

"Yes. Technically it's the only house, but my grandparents picked the number fifteen because it was the day they got married."

Rita's eyes traveled up and down Penny as joy chased surprise from her gently lined face. "You're Jonathan and Roberta Devonses' granddaughter?"

It was Penny's turn to be surprised. "You knew my grandparents?"

"Of course I did. I was born and raised in Deadwood. *Everyone* knew them." Rita abandoned her post at the computer in favor of perching on a cushioned stool she pulled out from under the counter's eave. "Your mama and I went to school together all the way through high school. We were friends—good friends. How is she? Is she here with you?"

Penny felt the instant well of tears born on the woman's questions and did her best to blink them away. "My mom passed away at the end of August. After a long illness."

"Oh sweetheart, I'm so sorry to hear that." Rita reached for Penny's hand and held it warmly between her own. "Kate was one of a kind."

"She was," Penny whispered past the tightening in her throat.

"And your daddy? I never met him, but Roberta raved about him when he and Kate got engaged."

Penny slipped her hand from between Rita's and thrust it inside the front pocket of her jeans. "My father passed away when I was four."

The woman's gasp left Penny shifting from foot to foot in an attempt to keep her composure. Her efforts proved futile, though, when Rita stepped out from behind the counter and enveloped Penny in her surprisingly strong arms.

Seconds turned to minutes as Penny gave in to the tears. She cried for the grandparents she knew only through stories. She cried for the father she didn't really remember. She cried for the mother she adored. And she cried for herself.

And through all of it, Rita quietly rubbed her back until Penny finally stepped away, emotionally spent. "I'm sorry. I don't usually make a habit of falling apart on complete strangers."

"First, don't ever apologize for loving someone with your whole heart." Rita pushed a lock of dampened hair off Penny's cheek and then grabbed hold of her hand once again. "And second, I'm *not* a complete stranger. I loved your mama too. Because before I met and married my husband, Tom, Kate Devons was my very best friend. Life and miles can't erase that."

Penny took the tissue Rita handed her and blew her nose. Then she frowned. "I don't remember my mom ever mentioning a Rita from her childhood."

"She wouldn't have. When I was growing up, people knew me more by my middle name, Anne."

"Wait. You're *Anne*?" Penny asked. "As in *that* Anne?"

Rita laughed. "You've heard the stories, I see."

"Tons."

"Hence, the switch to my given name once I became an adult." A mischievous glint sparkled in her eyes. "I'm teasing. Your mom and I were good kids. I just got to a point where I was tired of filling out forms as Rita and then having to correct people when they called me that. Seemed easier just to finally give in."

"Makes sense."

Rita nodded. "Do you have any siblings, sweetheart?"

"No. It's just me."

She hated the pity she saw in the woman's face. Not because she'd didn't feel it for herself at times too, but because it threatened to strip her of any and all strength she'd managed to convince herself she had. Desperate to keep that from happening, Penny willed herself to breathe, to square her shoulders, to think forward. "My mom left me the key to the house when she passed, and I decided to take a much-needed break from my job to come spend a little time in it. Only..." She stopped. Shook her head.

"Only three decades, give or take, have taken their toll on the place," Rita finished for her as she once again made her way back around the counter to the computer and Penny's list. "I remember watching your grandfather build all sorts of stuff when I was over there playing with your mama. He used to whistle the whole time he was working. Sometimes he'd see if we could guess what song he was whistling. Right this minute I can't remember anything he made, but I do remember that whatever he made, he made well. So I'm quite sure the bones of that house are as solid as can be, and the items on your list will be more about shoring up than redoing."

"From your mouth to God's ears," Penny murmured.

Rita's fingers paused on the keyboard just long enough to pin Penny with a knowing look. "He will guide you if you let Him."

"I'm trying."

"Faith has gotten me through many hardships in life—the death of my parents, a difficult birth with my first child, Lisa, and trying times here at the hardware store." Rita finished typing and leaned across the counter toward Penny, her eyes bright. "You have your mama's blond hair and that same little spray of freckles across the bridge of your nose. But those brilliant blue eyes? Those are your grandfather's, for sure."

Penny smiled. "That's what my mom always said."

"And your name is Penny, right?" Rita asked.

Penny felt her brows lift. "Yes. Penny McCormick. But how could you know that?"

"Kate settled on that name for you when we were just eight years old and playing house with our baby dolls."

"My mom picked out my name when she was eight?" Penny echoed.

Rita nodded. "She said your nickname would be Pennykins."

"It is. Wow," Penny said. "I didn't know that."

"She also said, way back then, that you'd be a beautiful girl. And you are."

Penny felt her cheeks warm at the praise. "Thank you."

"I imagine you have a special someone in your life?"

"No."

Rita's eyes brightened. "Well, well, well… Faith strikes again."

"Faith?" Penny echoed.

"Indeed."

It was on the tip of her tongue to question Rita's statement, but, in the end, she simply followed the woman's beckoning finger toward the various supplies on her list that she *could* fit in the car.

Paintbrushes.

Sandpaper.

Tape.

Nails.

Screws.

A hammer.

A power screwdriver.

And various shades of paint.

By the time everything was on the counter and the tab tallied, Penny was more than ready to track down something to eat at the sandwich shop Rita recommended on the east end of Main Street. With any luck, the energy boost from the food would carry through to the tasks she hoped to get to that afternoon.

"It was lovely to meet you, Penny. My youngest son, Seth, will be out at your place with the rest of your supplies not long after we close up here."

"What time do you close?" Penny asked.

"We're open every day except Sunday, ten to five."

Penny glanced at the clock on the wall, mentally calculated her available window, and then embraced her mother's childhood friend. "Thank you, Rita. For everything."

"You're very welcome, dear. And remember, be on the lookout for Seth." Rita stole a second hug and then stepped back to assess Penny with an added sparkle in her chocolate-brown eyes. "He doesn't have anyone special in his life yet either."

ᘓ Chapter Three ᘖ

She was tackling the last of the cobwebs when she heard a firm knock followed by the creak of the front door. "Hello? Miss McCormick? I have a delivery for you from Foster's Hardware."

"Oh, right. Yes, I'll be right with you." Wiping her hands down the sides of her jeans, Penny made her way across the web-free den and into the hallway. "Thank you for—"

The word *coming* stuck in her throat as her gaze fell on the sun-bleached brunette drinking her in from around the partially open door. A good six inches taller than Penny's own five-foot-five frame, Rita's son boasted the kind of tan that was produced only from spending long, sustained periods of time outdoors. His muscled arms spoke to the heavy lifting she imagined came with loading and unloading trucks with plywood and drywall and a bevy of tools and equipment for various DIY projects.

A sudden awareness of her sweat-soaked clothes and disheveled ponytail in relation to his simple yet clean Foster's Hardware shirt and his neatly groomed hair warmed her already-warm face even more as she worked to recover some semblance of her usual poise. "I guess it's after five?"

His second once-over left her shifting from foot to foot as, once again, she found herself wishing for a shower and a mirror. "It is." His amber-flecked brown eyes dipped briefly down to his wristwatch and then returned to meet her continued gaze along with a smile. "Five thirty, in fact."

"Clearly there were even more cobwebs than I realized, but at least I got them all."

He pushed the door open the rest of the way to pluck a silky strand from the part of her ponytail draped in front of her left shoulder. "*Almost* all of them," he corrected as he shook the webbed strand off his fingers onto a bandana he pulled from the front pocket of his well-fitting jeans.

With the last of the webbing finally gone, he thrust his hand in her direction and flashed a dimpled smile as she reciprocated. "I'm Seth, by the way. Seth Foster. My mom said this is your grandparents' place?"

"It is…was." She was surprised at the hesitation she felt as she leaned her tired body against the wall at her side. "They left it to my mom, who left it to me."

"Then I suppose a welcome to Deadwood is in order." Hooking his thumb across his shoulder toward the door, his expression took on a quizzical note that tugged his thick brows low. "I didn't see a moving van out front. Is that coming later? After you've gotten everything squared away in here?"

"No. No moving van. There's enough furniture here to get by for the time being. Especially since I'm not going to be living here full-time."

"Oh?"

"I have a condo in Tennessee, just outside of Knoxville. *This* place—if I can get it in order—will be a place to visit, on occasion, and to rent out on one of those vacation sites the rest of the time."

Seth stiffened. "You mean like to strangers?"

"That's right."

"How often?"

Parting company with the wall, she shrugged. "Ideally, I'd have this place filled every moment I'm not here, but that remains to be seen. From what I saw while driving in this morning and then again when I drove into town to your family's store, this is more of a get-away-from-life kind of place. The kind of spot that appeals to those wanting peace and quiet rather than a super touristy spot for their vacation. Fortunately, as I well know from my job, there's as big a market for the former as there is for the latter."

"Deadwood is a small town, Miss McCormick. Always has been."

"Call me Penny, please. And yes, I know. I grew up on stories about this place and its many charms, and I look forward to exploring it more before I have to head home later this month. But three, three-and-a-half weeks, should be plenty of time to get this place fixed up and to soak up the town where my grandparents met and fell in love so many years ago."

"If they loved it so much, why would you try to ruin it?"

His question slapped her back. "What am I trying to ruin?"

"Deadwood."

"How am I trying to ruin Deadwood?"

"By bringing in a parade of strangers who don't care a hoot about this town or the people who live in it."

"I'm not doing that," she argued, placing her hands on her hips.

"Will you know every one of the people who stay in this place when you're not here?"

"Of course not."

"Then that would make them strangers, wouldn't it?" He stepped back toward the door, only to stop, his formerly pleasant demeanor rapidly morphing into something resembling disgust. At her. "Strangers who'll leave their trash on our trails, drive too fast on our streets, and make it so those of us who live here will have to wait in longer lines at the sandwich shop or for a table at Franny's."

"That's a mighty big assumption, Seth."

"Are you saying it's out of the question? For each and every person who stays here?"

"I can't say for certain, but there are rules to follow and consequences if they're broken."

"Inside the walls of this house, maybe. But not in town. Not in our parks."

"That's rather pessimistic, don't you think?"

Raking his hand through his hair, he blew out a breath. "More like realistic, I'd say."

"Do you realize the kind of money vacationers bring to towns all over this country every year? And what those dollars can mean to a local economy? It's significant, Seth."

He palmed his mouth only to let his hand fall to his side in frustration. "And you know this because…?"

"Because I'm a freelance travel writer, and I research this stuff all the time."

"Deadwood is fine just the way it is. The way it's always been. And from what I've heard, that's the way your grandparents would want it to stay."

"So you're an expert on the feelings and beliefs of people you've never met?" she retorted.

Rolling his eyes, he again gestured toward the door with his thumb. "I think it's best if I bring in those supplies you ordered now."

"I agree." There was no disguising the anger in her voice and, frankly, she didn't care. Seth Foster might be good-looking, but he was nothing like his warm and welcoming mother.

Without another word, he led the way outside to a white pickup truck bearing the Foster's Hardware name and logo on the side panel. Inside the opened flatbed was the much-needed Weed eater, gardening implements, and various components for the projects she was confident she could take on by herself.

Together, they unpacked the items from the truck and stowed them in suitable places based on their intended task—lawn and garden equipment on the front porch, everything else in the front hallway. When all was in its proper place, Seth rocked on the heels of his work boots and pinned her with a wary eye. "Is there anything I can help you with before I head out?"

Oh, how she wanted to say no, to be rid of his judgmental silence once and for all, but the truth was, she did need his help with one thing.

"If you don't mind, there's a loose floorboard in one of the rooms that I can't seem to tighten back down. It might be a case of warping, or it might be a case of needing a bit more strength than I have."

He motioned for her to lead the way and then trailed behind her as she did. When she reached the troublesome spot, she knelt, demonstrated the board's looseness, and then glanced up at Seth. "See?"

With little more than a brisk nod and a knowing grunt, he squatted beside her, grabbed the hammer she'd left lying a few feet away, and gently pried the board upward until it was completely dislodged. Leaning forward, he tugged on the floor joist. "Looks to me like it was loosened on purpose."

She too leaned forward, her gaze hitting on a dark brown leather-bound book with the name *Johnathan Devonshire* embossed in gold lettering in the bottom right corner. "Jonathan Devonshire?" Penny murmured as she reached inside and recovered the book.

Seth hammered the board back into place and then nudged his chin toward Penny's hands. "Does that name mean something to you?"

"Part of it does."

"Meaning?"

"It's almost the same as my grandfather's name," she said, fingering the letters. "Only he was Jonathan Devons, not Devonshire."

"Interesting."

"I think so too." She started to open the book but stopped. There would be time to look at its contents later, after Seth was gone.

Rising, she reached her non-book-holding hand into her back pocket, pulled out a twenty-dollar bill, and handed it to Seth. "Thank you for bringing everything out and for finding"—she held up the book—"this. I really appreciate it."

"No problem." With a hesitance she argued against, Seth took the money and slipped it into his pocket. "Same-day delivery is just part of living in a small town like Deadwood."

"And staying to help with something like fixing a loose floor-board? Is that part of small-town life too?"

"It is, I suppose. But in this case, I suspect it was as much about my mom being up to her old tricks as anything else."

Something about his words and the way he said them on the heels of a slow head shake brought Penny up short. "Her old tricks?" she echoed. "Regarding what?"

"Regarding something that isn't going to happen no matter how much she might wish it would."

Before she could question him further, he uttered a less than heartfelt goodbye and made his way back out to his truck.

Chapter Four

It was nearly eleven o'clock by the time Penny sank onto the well-worn but oh-so-cozy couch. The house was a far cry from where it needed to be in order to be listed with a vacation rental company, but she was making progress. Little by little. Tomorrow, she'd get at it again with a fresh pair of eyes and a body that—hopefully—had rebounded after a decent night's sleep.

Her legs were tired. Her arms were tired. Her feet were tired. In fact, every part of her body was tired. Except her brain. That had been bouncing her back and forth between whatever task she'd been tackling in the moment and the frustrating man that was Rita Foster's son. Yes, he was handsome. Yes, he'd been helpful. But really, what business did he have voicing an opinion on her plans for her family's home? And how on earth could someone who relied on his income from a small business be so ignorant about the potential benefits from new blood coming and going in Deadwood?

Releasing a breath of frustration, Penny wandered her eyes around the family room that had once been the heart of her grandparents' home. The stone fireplace centered against the exterior wall was what she'd expect from the 1950s with its heavy wooden mantel and wide hearth. She knew, from childhood stories her mom had told, that the three nails jutting out from the mantel's front edge were where the family's stockings had been hung on

Christmas Eve each year. And the spot directly above the middle one had been where the manger had sat, waiting for her mom to place the baby Jesus inside it before heading to bed that night. She tried to imagine the stockings and the manger, the perfect live Christmas tree they'd settle on—and decorate!—together in the weeks leading up to the holiday, and the love and laughter she knew had surrounded all of it.

She knew it, because it was the same experience her mother had made sure Penny had growing up. Only instead of it being there, in Deadwood, it had been in the condo Penny had lived in with her own parents. Even after her dad's accident, her mom had determined to make Penny's life special by maintaining treasured traditions while creating new memories along the way.

Feeling the familiar loneliness begin to descend across her entire being, Penny willed herself to think of something, anything, to keep from going down a mental path that would make it so she couldn't sleep. Sleep was her only escape from a reality she simply wasn't ready to embrace yet, if ever. And when she wasn't sleeping, staying busy was the ticket—something that shouldn't be difficult to do in light of the house's current condition.

That said, the cobwebs were gone, the kitchen had been scrubbed from top to bottom, the first coat of paint in the bathroom was virtually dry, and the loose floorboard had been successfully tightened thanks to—

Penny sat up, craned her neck toward the back left corner of the couch, and pulled the brown, leather-bound notebook onto her lap. Slowly, almost reverently, she ran the tips of her fingers along the soft cover and across the gold-leafed name at the bottom—a name so similar to her grandfather's she couldn't help but take notice. Especially when it was found, tucked away from sight, in the house her grandfather had built by hand.

Curious, she walked her fingers to the cover's edge and opened it, her gaze falling on an inscription written in the most beautiful calligraphy she'd ever seen.

My dearest Jonathan,

There are no words for the pain I feel over your decision to leave Chicago, but I understand. Anyone who doesn't value the generous and kindhearted young man you are doesn't deserve to walk this life with you no matter who they are or how right they may seem on the surface.

You are deserving of someone who sees and knows you for who you truly are. And I know that one day, when the time is right, you will find that person. Of that, I have no doubt. When you do, please be yourself. Show her the man I know you to be, the one you've always been for anyone who cared to see beyond the matching exterior.

I also know that to deny your ability as a carpenter will only spite yourself. Don't do that. You took to your father's world like a duck to water. That's not a judgment or a statement made to induce guilt, but, rather, a simple truth. Still, I hope you will always find a way to let your ability with pen and paper be a part of your life, as it's as much a part of you as your soul.

Let this book be the place where you allow yourself to nurture that gift while making your own way in this world.

Never, ever, forget how much I love you and how endlessly blessed I've been to be your mother.
 Always and forever proud of my son,
 Mom

It was the kind of letter Penny's mom might have written to Penny. Encouraging, praising, uplifting. It also left her thinking, wondering...

The Jonathan who'd owned this book had to be her grandfather. It was the only thing that made sense. Chicago was a big city, even in—she took in the date next to her great-grandmother's inscription—*1950*, and her mother had always said Grandpa Jon had big-city roots. And the carpentry part? Penny only had to look around the room to know the family patriarch had been skilled. The evidence was everywhere.

But the writing part? That was the only thing that didn't—

"If your grandfather were alive today, Pennykins, he'd be positively tickled that you've chosen writing as your career."

The sudden explosion of her mother's voice inside her head tumbled Penny's thoughts back to the day she had graduated from college. She remembered the hotter-than-normal temperatures, the countless pictures taken with friends, and the excitement she'd felt as she walked across the stage to receive her diploma while her mother's cheers rang out from somewhere deep inside the stadium. But more than all of that, she remembered the genuine pride she'd seen on her mother's face while uttering that very sentence after the ceremony—a sentence Penny now realized she'd never explored.

All her life, her grandparents and her father had been kept alive in her mind and heart through her mother's anecdotes and memories. Sometimes they'd taken the form of bedtime stories, sometimes they'd been delivered up to help pass the time in a doctor's office or on a long car ride, and sometimes they'd found their way into teaching moments as Penny was growing up.

She'd always assumed she'd absorbed them all, but had she? Had there really come a point when she'd stopped listening? Stopped hearing?

Feeling suddenly unsettled, Penny ran her hand down the inscription one more time and then moved on to the next page. There, in what could only be described as more manly penmanship, was a poem about life and change and wanting something different. Each word choice, each image created, made her stop. Think. Feel.

Next, came an essay about passion. At first, it seemed the passion referenced was for a thing. Then, maybe a person. Or life. Or maybe all of the above. Whatever it was, it was so beautifully written it stole her breath in several spots.

Page by page, she made her way through the first half of the book, reading more poems and more essays before hitting upon a piece far more journal-like than any of the others. The handwriting was still the same, if not perhaps a little more rushed than that of the previous pages.

A tree came down behind the house yesterday. Didn't hurt anything, but it'll take time to clear. When I came across it after the storm, it got me thinking about roots. A tree with strong roots—the kind that dig deep into the ground

together—fares better in storms because it's hardier. A tree
with shallow roots—the kind that seem to meander with no
real purpose—tends to be the first one to fall in tough times.
That's a lot like families, isn't it?

The nature of the piece suggested it had been written during a
more reflective mood, and Penny found that it made her thoughts
wander as well. She'd grown up hearing story after story about her
grandparents' courtship and marriage, her mother's childhood in
Deadwood, the love story that was her grandparents' life together,
and bits and pieces about Grandma Roberta's family. Yet, surprisingly, she knew nothing about her grandfather's kin and, until that
moment, she'd never really given it much thought.

She pondered that against what he'd written and then moved on,
continuing her way through the rest of the leather-bound tome filled
with poetry, stories, and the occasional observation about life. A few
pages from the end, she came across a familiar black-and-white photograph tucked discreetly in the book's spine. In this one, unlike its
near carbon copy that had been framed and displayed in her childhood home, her grandfather was standing instead of sitting, the
reflective expression she'd all but memorized over the years replaced
by a devilish grin that stretched his full-lipped mouth wide.

It was funny how something as simple as standing versus sitting
and smiling versus thinking could project such a striking difference
in the same person, but it could, and it did. The man in the framed
picture on her mother's mantel had always made Penny feel warm
and safe, whereas this version brought her none of the warm fuzzies
she associated with her grandfather.

She made a mental note to take a more critical look at her work-related headshots the next time she was on the computer and then flipped the page, her gaze, once again, coming to rest on her grandfather's handwriting.

> *I ran.*
> *I told myself it was because I felt trapped.*
> *I told myself it was so I could live my own life.*
> *I told myself change was necessary.*
> *I told myself there was no other way.*
> *But the simple truth is that I ran out of fear of the steel bars certain to be my destiny if I had stayed.*
> *I am a coward.*
> *I am a coward living life in the shadow of his own lie.*

Intrigued, she flipped to the next page, anxious to read more. Yet, despite the presence of a good half dozen more pages before the end of the book, there was nothing.

Had Grandpa Jon been thinking about writing a novel? Testing rhythm and flow for a new poem? Or had he just been ramble-writing?

Writers were funny that way. Words and sentences were their version of an artist's doodling. When she was on the phone with an editor, when she was dreaming about locales to write about, when she was fantasizing about the women's fiction novel that had been knocking at her muse for longer than she could remember, she ramble-wrote.

It was something she gave such little thought to most days, but sitting there, soaking up the writings of a man she'd never met, it made her feel a part of something bigger than any one moment or any one place.

With a last look at her grandfather's handwriting, Penny flipped the book closed and allowed herself not one, but two big yawns. It had been a long day. An exhausting day. But as disappointing as her first glance of the house had been, she was glad she'd stayed. This place had been special to her mother, and that alone made her want to know its every nook and cranny.

She wanted to eat where her mother and grandparents had eaten. She wanted to sleep where her mother had slept. She wanted to read on the same window seat where her mom had fallen in love with books. And maybe, just maybe, she wanted to do a little writing in a place where her grandfather had written too.

Slowly, gently, Penny smoothed her hand across the book's soft leather cover to the ribbony placeholder she'd failed to tuck inside. To the gold-lettered name in which four letters had mistakenly been added to—

Penny bolted upright on the couch so hard and so fast that the book slipped off her lap and onto the floor with a hard thump. Leaning over, she stared at the open page and its hastily written words.

> *I ran.*
> *I told myself it was because I felt trapped.*
> *I told myself it was so I could live my own life.*
> *I told myself change was necessary.*
> *I told myself there was no other way.*
> *But the simple truth is that I ran out of fear of the steel bars certain to be my destiny if I had stayed.*

I am a coward.

I am a coward living life in the shadow of his own lie.

Those words weren't the beginning of a novel. Nor were they a test of rhythm or flow for a poem or song. No, they were exactly what they sounded like—an admission of wrongdoing by a man who'd done something worthy of jail time, who fled the scene for some blip-on-the-map town in Oregon and dropped four letters from the end of his name to avoid being discovered.

If it had been the setup of a present-day mystery novel, Penny might have laughed. But it wasn't a mystery novel. And it wasn't just some throw-away character from the pre-internet era. It was real.

All her life she'd been raised to know her grandfather as a man of honesty and integrity, the kind of man who doted on his family and stood strong in his faith. But now? After what he'd written? After what he'd hidden?

"Oh, Grandpa Jon," Penny whispered. "What did you do?"

CHAPTER FIVE

She'd just finished cleaning the second window and was moving on to the third and final one along the rear wall of the house when she heard the telltale thud of a truck's gate. Outside her condo in Tennessee, it wasn't a sound that stuck out. But here, against a backdrop reigned by chirping birds and scurrying squirrels, its effect wasn't much different than a sudden dousing of frigid water.

Wiping her hands on the cleaning rag, Penny poked her head around the side of the house and noted the same Foster's Hardware pickup truck from the previous evening. "Hello?" she called out. "I'm around back."

"I see that."

Penny whirled to find Seth coming around the other side of the house with a stepstool in one hand and a toolbox in the other. "You scared me to death!"

"Why? You just said you were back here." Seth leaned the stepstool in the space between the two freshly cleaned windows and set the toolbox in front of his feet. "And, so, here I am."

She hooked a thumb over her shoulder. "I expected you'd come around that way."

"There's more than one way to skin a cat, yes?"

"What a lovely thought," she murmured before pointing at the new additions to her yard. "I knew about the stepstool, seeing as how I called in that order when you opened this morning, but the toolbox? I didn't order one of those."

"You wanted help around here, right?" The amber flecks in Seth's eyes glistened in the sun as he took inventory of her completed tasks thus far that morning. When he reached the window she'd yet to do, he crossed his arms, clearly waiting for her to speak.

She, in turn, stared at him, thrown. "I asked your mom if she knew anyone I could hire, but I didn't know she was going to send *you*."

"And yet here I am."

"But it's the middle of the workday. Doesn't she need you at the store?"

"Most likely, yes. But not as much as she wants me out here. With you."

"Come again?" Penny tossed the rag onto the bucket she'd found in a storage closet under the stairs. "I didn't follow that."

He glanced up at the sky, pulled a ball cap from his toolbox, and tugged it down over his head until just the tiniest hint of hair was visible around its bottom edge. "It *is* the middle of the workday. Yes, my mother probably needs me at the store. And no, no amount of work that needs to be done there was going to sway her from the opportunity your request afforded."

"Opportunity?" she echoed. "What opportunity?"

"For help."

She tried to make sense of what Seth was saying, but after yesterday's long drive to get there and the restless night of sleep in the wake of her grandfather's troubling words, she felt as if he were speaking a foreign language. "I asked for the names of some handymen, that's all," she said.

"I'm sure you did. But my mom has a one-track mind these days when it comes to me and my future. And, well…" He crouched, ran his fingers along an exterior board, and shrugged. "She sees you as the one who just might change things for me."

"*I* might change things for *you*? How could—" And then she knew. It was there in the boredom lapping at the edges of his voice. It was there in the fatigue emanating off his being. And, yeah, looking back to the previous day, it had been there in the way Rita had talked about Seth as Penny was preparing to leave the store. "Oh no."

"Oh yes."

"But she just met me," Penny protested. "Yesterday. For a grand total of about twenty—maybe thirty—minutes."

Seth walked a few steps closer to Penny and, again, crouched down to inspect another stretch of the same board. "That doesn't matter," he said, his tone and his demeanor unaffected by the subject matter at hand. "You're the first visually appealing, like-aged woman to walk into our store without a wedding ring in over a year. That's huge."

Visually appealing?

Before she could truly digest his description of her and how easily it rolled off his tongue, he reached into his box for a hammer and nail. "Add to that the fun fact that you're related to some sort of early town royalty and, well, you get the picture of what we're up against here."

After reclaiming the bottle of window cleaner from its resting spot beneath the final window, Penny squirted the glass with quick, jerky movements. "As far as the royalty part is concerned, it's looking like that won't be the case for much longer."

He paused his hammering to look up at Penny. "Well, that's mighty cryptic."

"Tell me about it." She wiped away the decades-old grime to reveal her own sun-reflected image. In the shadows under the blue eyes she shared with her grandfather, she saw the heartache of the past few months. In the dip of her shoulders, she saw the fatigue that came with trying to stay positive amid the soul-crushing loneliness that was her life now. And in the lip she worried on and off between her teeth, she saw uncertainty—about her present, her future, and now, thanks to her grandfather's journal, her past too.

"You suddenly look like you lost your best friend or something. You okay?"

She abandoned her own reflection in favor of Seth's. "Me? Yeah, I'm…fine. Just a little tired, I guess."

"I take it you worked into the night?"

She squirted the last section of the window and began to wipe, grateful for the opportunity to get back on more solid ground. "I painted the bathroom and cleaned and scoured the kitchen and then prepped the walls for the painting I plan to get to later today."

"No moss grows on you, I see." He returned the hammer to his toolbox only to retrieve it, once again, as he spied another spot that needed securing. "So, did you get a chance to check out that book?"

Stilling her hand mid-wipe, she stared at the man just over her right shoulder. "Book?"

"Yeah, the one that was under that loose floorboard I fixed."

Right. She'd forgotten he'd been there to find it.

"I did." She finished the window and stepped back, the afternoon sun warm on her head. "Hey, do you happen to know if there are any marked trailheads around here?"

"Tons. Why? You like to hike?"

"I do. But really, I'm just trying to get a handle on what's around so I know how best to position this place when I'm finally ready to rent it out to vacationers. An extensive trail network would be a real selling point for the outdoorsy types."

He stopped hammering. "Did nothing I say yesterday make a difference to you at all?"

"Meaning?"

"This is a small town, Penny. By design. Folks around here like it that way."

She wiped away the last of the dirt. "Bringing in vacationers to *one* house isn't going to change that."

"Maybe. But how long before others around here start doing the same?"

"If everybody around here is as set on Deadwood staying exactly the way it is as you *say* they are, then you shouldn't have anything to worry about in that regard, correct?" She turned her full attention on Seth, noted the growing tension in his upper body, and then tossed her cleaning cloth into the bucket. "I suspect this whole issue is really more *your* hang-up than anyone else's."

He dropped the hammer back into his toolbox and shrugged. "I like living in a place where everyone knows each other. Just like my mom knew you…or rather, your family."

"That *was* kind of cool," she conceded.

"She not only knew your grandparents, she remembers them. Clearly. Shared some of her memories about them with me just this morning before she sent me here with the stepstool you ordered. I'd bet good money that running into someone who knew you, let alone your kin, wouldn't happen in some big vacation town."

It was a safe bet and one she couldn't argue. Instead, she let the part about his mom propel her to the front of the house and the painting she'd propped against the front porch railing earlier that morning. When Seth caught up, she pointed his attention to the canvas. "My grandmother painted that before I was born. It hung in our living room my whole life."

Seth stepped in for a closer look, his gaze taking in the same details Penny had all but memorized while silently comparing them with the structure in front of them at that moment. "It's held up quite well considering how long it's been vacant."

"I was told my grandfather was a gifted carpenter."

He nodded. "I take it you never met him?"

"No." She thought about the journal entry that had made it nearly impossible to sleep last night and willed a lightness into her voice she didn't feel. "Not in person, anyway. Grandpa Jon and Grandma Roberta both passed before I was born. But my mom did her best to keep them alive in her stories about growing up here in Deadwood. In this very house."

"Why did your mom leave Deadwood?"

Penny lowered herself onto the aging front step and stared out at her car parked beneath a canopy of trees along the edge of the dirt driveway. "She met my father in college, and he got a job right after graduation that had him needing to be in Knoxville. When he passed, I was just four years old. My mom believed consistency was important, so she opted to keep us right where we were."

"Makes sense," he said. "And she passed recently too?"

Penny stared at him, startled, only to look away as the memory of her trip to the hardware store the previous day took center stage in her thoughts. "She wanted me to come here, to see this place, to feel a…" She shook off the emotion gathering in her voice and stood. "Anyway, I should probably get back to work. Thank you for stopping by, and—"

"Have you driven around town much?"

She returned her attention to the handsome man lifting his toolbox into the bed of his truck. "I drove down Main Street yesterday to get to your family's hardware store. I saw the town hall, the fire station, the market, the ice cream shop, et cetera. And, on your mom's advice, I grabbed a sandwich at that place next to the library."

"How about the side streets and stuff? Explore any of those?"

"Not yet, no."

Seth looked at his wristwatch and then motioned toward his truck. "I could drive you around if you've got a few minutes?"

"I really can't. Too much stuff to do, and too little time to do it in."

He folded his arms across his muscled chest. "Don't you think you should know the place you're going to be pushing to people?"

"Of course, but—"

"Then let me show it to you."

"I thought you were against the idea of me renting this place out," she countered.

"I am."

She laughed. "Ah, I get it. You think you can change my mind, don't you?"

"There's no *think* about it." Dropping his hands to his sides, Seth nudged his chin toward his truck. "Thirty minutes is all I'm asking for. After that, I'll bring you home again."

A low growl from somewhere deep inside her stomach had her remembering the sandwich shop and its surprisingly robust menu from the previous day. "Fine. Make it twenty, with a stop at the sandwich place on our way back here, and you're on."

CHAPTER SIX

Road by road, Seth drove her around Deadwood, sharing details about the houses they passed and the families who called them home.

The Sandersons on Fork Road were a multigenerational family on the same land: great-grandparents in the white house, grandparents in the blue house, and parents and children in the maroon one. Seth's mother had gone to school with the grandmother.

Nathan Wright, on Lake Creek Mountain Road, was the town's mayor decades earlier. A widower upon the death of his wife, Lillian, the beloved man spent his days fishing in a small pond on his property.

Catherine and Max Welding, on Upper Deadwood Creek Road, had taught in the local school for more than thirty years. Both Rita and Seth had had Catherine for math, and Seth and his dad, Tom, had both had Max for shop class.

Twice, Seth stopped the car to exchange pleasantries with someone he spied out on a front lawn or walking along the street. And, in both cases, it was impossible to ignore his ease as he answered questions about his parents and siblings and asked a handful of his own about their families.

For the first fifteen minutes or so, Penny actually enjoyed the drive and Seth's accompanying narration. Eventually, though, she

felt her mood shifting from lighthearted to something more like...
sadness? She tried to cover it with well-timed nods and an occasional *hmm* for good measure, but when even that proved too much,
she let silence take over—a silence Seth seemed oblivious to as he
came to a stop in front of the sandwich shop.

"So?" He cut the engine and turned to Penny. "Impressions?
Thoughts? Comments?"

"No, not really."

Seth pulled the keys from the ignition and closed them in his
hand. "Oh, c'mon. Admit it. This idea of yours to rent your grandparents' house to total strangers just doesn't fit. Maybe in another
town it would. But not here. Not in Deadwood."

"So you'd rather I leave it the way it is?" she countered.
"Abandoned and being overtaken by weeds?"

"No. Of course not. I think you should just keep it for yourself."

She heard the sarcasm in her answering laugh. "For what
purpose?"

"To live in. Full-time."

"I can't do that," she protested.

"Why not? You said you're a freelancer."

Reaching down, Penny plucked her purse from its resting spot
beside her feet and began fiddling with the purse strap. "I am, but..."
She stopped. Shook her head. Wrapped her fingers around the passenger door handle. "I really need to get something to eat so you can get
me to the house and I can get back to my tasks. The clock is ticking."

"You're a freelancer but *what*?" he pressed.

Penny returned her hand to her purse strap and shrugged. "I
have a place. In Tennessee."

"Yeah, but your family is all gone now, right?"

Something about hearing her reality on someone else's lips was like a sucker punch to the stomach—one that left her struggling to think, let alone offer anything more than a terse nod.

"So there you go. Get rid of the place in Tennessee and live in your grandparents' house yourself."

She jerked her eyes up to his. "You're actually serious."

"Why wouldn't I be?" He drummed his fingers on the steering wheel. "Unless Deadwood isn't exciting enough for you?"

"No. It's beautiful. Peaceful."

His fingers stilled. "Then what's the problem?"

"I…" She looked back at the shop. Swallowed. "I don't fit here."

"Everyone fits here."

"That's not what you said a few minutes ago about vacation-home renters."

He blew out a breath, his exasperation evident. "Because they're not vested in Deadwood. They'll be in and out in a matter of days."

"Okay," she said, meeting and then abandoning his eyes once again. "And your point?"

"Did you hear anything I said when I was showing you around town just now? About the generations of families who live here? About the teachers who have taught grandparents and grandchildren from the same families? About the—"

"I heard. I saw." She heard the tremble in her voice despite her best effort to will it away. "That's why I wouldn't fit. I don't have that. Here or anywhere."

Silence filled the space between them for several long beats—beats that were finally broken by the sound of Seth clearing his throat and the feel of his hand as it closed on top of Penny's. "But don't you see, you *do* fit here. Your family came from here. My mom knew them, remembers them. I have no doubt others will as well."

"But what if they didn't really *know* them?" she asked, recovering her hand from beneath his. "In particular, my grandfather."

Seth shifted so his back was flush to the driver's side door and the entirety of his view was Penny. "There are lots of people in Deadwood who grew up with my mom. If she knew your grandfather, then so did they."

"That's not what I mean."

"Then help me understand what you *do* mean."

Should she?

Could—

"I don't think my grandfather was who he said he was," she blurted out.

Seth's eyebrow inched upward. "What do you mean?"

"That book we found under the floorboards last night? I'm almost certain it was his. Why would he change his name?"

Seth's shoulders fell in a slow, reflective shrug. "People did that sometimes back then, didn't they? To downplay an ethnicity or for basic ease?"

"Maybe. But what if he changed it because he was hiding something awful? Something he could've gotten in trouble for if people had known?"

His laugh was not unkind. "That's probably a bit of a leap, don't you think?"

"I want to think it's a leap. I really do. But…" She shrugged and looked out at the car parked in front of them.

"Talk to me, Penny."

"Based on the handwritten inscription inside, his mother—my great-grandmother, Vivian—gave that book to him. As a place for the poems and essays and stories he liked to write."

"Did you know he liked to write stuff like that before yesterday?" Seth asked.

"I knew he made up bedtime stories for my mom when she was little. And she told me how proud he would've been to know I'd become a writer. So, yeah, I guess it wasn't that much of a surprise."

"Did you read any of it?"

She closed her eyes. Counted to ten in her head. Opened her eyes in time with a deep inhale and an even deeper exhale. "I read all of it."

"And?"

"Most of it was poems and observations about life. You know, stuff like that. But then, the last thing he wrote was more journal-like." She felt the familiar prick of tears building in the corners of her eyes and did her best to blink them away. "He ran from something, Seth. Something big, I think. Something serious. And now I don't know what to think. I don't know, anymore, if all those stories I grew up hearing about my grandfather and the kind of man he was were even true. And if they *weren't* true, and he was actually on the run from something truly awful, then what? What does that make him? What does that make my grandmother? What does that make my mother? What does it make *me?*"

Leaning forward, he opened the glove box, extracted a small package of tissues, and handed one to Penny. "First off, if he ran from something, that has no bearing on anyone but him. *He* ran. Not you. Not your mom. Not your grandmother. So put that worry to rest right now. And anyway, maybe it wasn't a journal entry. Maybe it was just a story."

"That's what I thought at first too. That it was the opening of a novel he'd been playing with, or some sort of cadence exercise or something." Penny wiped her eyes. "But he altered his name, Seth. And he hid the book under a floorboard in his house."

He returned his hand to the steering wheel and tapped his fingers against it. "Right. Okay. That does make you wonder a little, doesn't it?"

"It makes me wonder a lot." She hurried to stifle the hiccup born from her tears. "All I have left of my mom and my dad are memories of them. And all I have left of my grandparents are the stories my mom told me. I—I don't want those to be wrong. They're all I have left of them. I need that."

"Maybe they're not wrong."

Penny lifted her watery gaze to Seth. "But what if they are? What then?"

For a moment, maybe two, he said nothing, his expression difficult to discern. When he finally spoke, though, it was with a gentleness and a compassion that grabbed hold of her heart like a warm, steadying hug. "Then we'll cross that bridge when we come to it. For now, let's get you fed and then go back to the house to tackle a few more items on your to-do list. Then, tomorrow, we'll put our heads together and figure out the best way to get you those answers about your grandfather."

"I'm scared," she admitted as she followed him onto the sidewalk. "I want him to be what he's always been—a man of strength and integrity."

At the door to the sandwich shop, Seth's hand found the small of her back and guided her inside. "I know. I want that for you too."

❧ CHAPTER SEVEN ❧

It was barely nine o'clock when Penny heard the sound of a car door slamming closed outside the house. Slipping her freshly washed ponytail through the hole in her ball cap, she peeked outside the kitchen window at the now familiar man making haste toward the front porch with a brown bag in one hand and his toolbox in the other.

There was no doubt about it. Seth Foster was a good-looking guy. His tanned and muscled arms spoke to the physical labor that was clearly part of his job at the hardware store. She knew, from snippets of conversation they'd had while prepping the kitchen walls for painting, that his duties at the store ran the gamut from customer service to unloading trucks as well as after-hours' deliveries to people in Deadwood and the surrounding towns. But the part of his job that lit up his eyes was doing exactly what he'd done for her the previous day—helping people with various do-it-yourself projects.

Stepping back from the window just enough to buy her a few more seconds of unnoticed gawking time, she took in his sure-footed gait, the way his sun-bleached brown hair curled ever so slightly around the edges of his ball cap, and the endearingly crooked smile he wore as he took the pair of porch stairs with a single giant step.

His low, rumbly voice drifted through the screen in conjunction with a knock. "Delivery for Miss McCormick."

"I didn't order anything," she yelled, grinning.

"Hmm. I must've read the address wrong when I was putting these fresh-from-the-oven blueberry muffins in the bag. My bad. Sorry for the inconven—"

Penny fairly ran to the door, only to find that the sound of his departing footsteps had clearly been a ruse. "Did you say blueberry muffins?" she asked, looking from Seth to the bag and back again.

"I did."

She licked her lips. "Fresh from the oven?"

"That's right."

"Actually, I think you have the right address after all."

His widening smile called his matching dimples into action. "Good answer."

Pushing open the door, Penny stepped to the side to afford Seth entry into the house and then led the way down the hall. At the doorway to the kitchen, she stopped and swept his attention toward the freshly painted walls. "So? What do you think?" she asked.

"Whoa. When did you do this?"

She stepped inside the small yet cozy space as she too took in the totality of the room. "Yesterday, after you left. I figured we'd prepped the walls, so why not?"

"It looks great." He crossed to the table, set his toolbox beneath it and the bag of muffins on top of it, and gave the walls another, longer, once-over. "You're right. The pale yellow was a good choice."

"Thank you. I'm quite happy with the way it came out."

"One more thing off your to-do list," he said.

"One more thing." She stepped over to the drawer next to the sink, pulled out a stack of napkins, and handed them to Seth. "Unfortunately, I've been a little too busy to do much shopping, so all I've got to offer you to drink is water."

"Water works." A moment later he took the glass of ice water she offered, set it on the table, and waited for Penny to pick a chair. When she did, he reached into the bag and extracted a muffin for her and one for himself. Instead of taking a bite of his own, though, he leaned back in his chair and motioned for her to start.

Penny took a bite and— "Whoa. This is… This is *incredible*." She looked down at the muffin and the generous helping of blueberries peeking out around her lone bite. "Are these from the coffee shop in town, or did Rita make them?"

"If I were a lesser man I would take offense to the second part of that question."

She took another bite and another, aware of little else besides the explosion of flavor in her mouth. On the fourth or fifth bite, her brain finally caught up with his words and she found herself staring at him across the table. "Wait. Are you saying that *you* made these?"

"I am, and I did." He lifted his muffin into the air, toast-like, and then took a bite.

Again, she looked at what was left of her muffin. "From your mother's recipe?"

"Nope. From my own."

"Seriously?"

His dimples on full display, he nodded.

"Wow. Just…*wow*. They're fantastic." She finished her muffin, finger-fed herself a stray crumb, and then sank back in her chair. "When did you come up with that recipe?"

He shrugged. Finished his own muffin. Collected his napkin and hers and balled them up inside his hand. "Every Sunday morning after church, my family comes together for a big brunch—my parents, my siblings and their spouses, my nieces and nephew, and me. It's just something we do. For the longest time, it was always at Mom and Dad's house. Mom would make pancakes, and Dad would make bacon or sausage. Eventually, when my sisters and brother got married and moved out, they wanted to help lighten my mother's load by hosting a Sunday morning brunch of their own. My sister, Lisa, took one Sunday. My other sister, Dana, took another Sunday, and my brother, Doug, and his wife, Lila, took another. And just as Mom and Dad had always made pancakes, Lisa's turn became synonymous with cinnamon rolls, Dana's with waffles, and Doug and Lila's with French toast.

"When I moved out on my own, I felt it was only right for me to take a Sunday morning slot too. And since I didn't want to duplicate what any of the others did, I figured I needed to come up with something else. So, after much trial and error with various cookbook recipes for blueberry muffins, I went rogue and came up with my own."

"My mom and I did something like that," Penny shared in a voice that was little more than a whisper. "Only our thing was every Friday night."

He leaned forward. "Tell me about it."

And so she did.

She told him about their guilty pleasure of bypassing dinner in favor of dessert every Friday night.

She told him about the laughter they'd shared over failed recipes and the high fives they exchanged when they found a keeper.

She told him about the game they'd made of who-could-find-the-cutest-paper-plates for dessert night each week.

And, in a trembling voice, she told him about the last dessert night they'd shared before her mother's passing and how Penny had made every single one of their favorites.

"That sounds mighty special," Seth said. "*Mighty* special."

"It was the best," Penny echoed. "*She* was the best. And I miss her more than I can say."

"I'm sorry."

She tried to swallow away the lump rising in her throat, but when it wouldn't budge, she cleared it the best she could with a cough. "Me too."

For several long minutes they sat in silence. Eventually, Seth pushed back his chair and stood. "I'm not sure if anything will come of it, but I thought of someone who might be able to shed a little light on your grandfather—if you're up to it?"

Startled, Penny looked up at Seth. "Who?"

"Her name is Glenda. Glenda Farmer. She turned a hundred this past spring. She isn't getting around quite as fast as she used to, but her mind is still sharp as a tack."

"And you think she knew my grandfather?"

"I know she did," said Seth. "Her husband was the foreman at Deadwood Lumber where, according to my mom, your grandfather worked."

Penny scooted back her chair and stood, all thoughts of blueberry muffins and being alone temporarily sidelined. "Oh, I'm most definitely up for this."

Despite her advanced age, Glenda Farmer was clearly a force to be reckoned with if the slow, thorough once-over she was giving Penny at that moment was any indication. Surprisingly though, Penny didn't find it the least bit unsettling. Instead, she simply waited out the inspection from her spot on the couch next to Seth and returned the smile she finally got with one of her own.

"It's not that often we see a new face in Deadwood, particularly one as pretty as yours." Glenda's eyes, magnified behind her bifocals, traveled left to Seth. "Your mother's prayers must be working, young man."

In a different circumstance, the centenarian's comment would have flamed Penny's cheeks as red as Seth's, but in that moment, Penny's thoughts were singularly focused on one thing: getting answers.

"My grandparents actually lived here in Deadwood for many years." When Glenda's full attention was back on Penny, Penny continued. "Raised my mom here too. Right up until she went to college."

The elderly woman tilted her head to the left and then the right as, once again, she studied Penny. "Well, well, well… You're Roberta Devons's granddaughter, aren't you?"

Pleased, Penny sat up tall. "I am."

"You have her same high cheekbones and the same faint freckling across the bridge of your nose. And your eyes? They're the same blue as Jonathan's. I'm surprised I didn't put two and two together right away." Glenda ran her long, bony fingers across the armrests of her chair and then dropped them into her lap. "Did your mother come with you?"

"No. My mother passed at the end of August."

Glenda's soft tsking echoed in the otherwise silent room. "I'm sorry to hear that, dear. Your mother was a special one."

Penny blinked. Looked away. "She was. I miss her every minute of every day."

"And the one who stole her heart while she was off at college?"

"My father died when I was four."

"Do you have any siblings?"

She shook her head. "No. It's just me."

"We have that in common, I see." Glenda turned her attention back to Seth. "So, what brings you to my door today, young man?"

Seth pointed at Penny. "Penny and I were hoping you might be able to answer some questions about her grandfather."

"Oh?"

Penny nodded. "I understand your husband hired my grandfather at the lumber mill when he first came to Deadwood."

"That's right."

"Is there anything you can tell me about him when he first came here? Any references he might've given or details about his life your husband might've shared with you?"

Glenda reached up and adjusted her glasses. "I met your grandfather shortly after Roland hired him. I found him to be rather sullen in those early days."

"Sullen?" Penny echoed.

"I remember trying to make conversation with him one day while I was waiting for Roland to finish up his work. I asked your grandfather about his life in Chicago."

Penny exchanged glances with Seth and then matched his lean forward on the couch. "And? What did he say?"

"He changed the subject."

"Did you ever try again?" Seth asked.

"Of course I did. I couldn't let something like that go."

Penny waited for more, but when Glenda stayed silent, she asked the only question she could. "And? Did he ever tell you anything about his life before Deadwood?"

"No, he did not. He changed the subject every single time. And he changed it *fast*." Glenda shifted in her seat. "Which ended up being a good life lesson for me about the dangers of snap judgments."

"Meaning?" Penny prodded.

"I was convinced your grandfather was on the run from something. Even told Roland he better watch the till."

Penny felt the weight of Seth's gaze, but she couldn't meet it. "On the run from something?"

"Why else would he keep mum about where he'd come from?" Glenda posed. "But, in the end, Jonathan Devons proved himself to be a good man here in Deadwood. And really, isn't that all that matters in the end?"

Oh, how she wanted to share that sentiment, to focus on the man he was when he was married to her grandmother and the father he'd been to her own mother, but the nagging uncertainty of what might have been simply wouldn't let go. "Does that mean you no longer think he was hiding something all those years ago?"

"No. I still think that," Glenda said on the heels of a yawn. "Always have, always will. But it's only a guess. The only one who knew for sure was your grandfather, and he's long gone."

CHAPTER EIGHT

"You okay?"

Somehow, Penny made herself nod. It was the least she could do, considering the block of time Seth had given from his day to try to help. But in reality, she wasn't okay.

"Talk to me," he said, backing down Glenda's driveway and out onto the road.

She felt him shift into drive, saw Glenda's house decrease in size in the sideview mirror, and then rested her temple against the passenger-side window. "What's to say? Apart from the obvious."

"Which is?"

"Any miniscule shred of hope I may have quietly harbored as to a positive reason my grandfather wrote what he wrote is gone. Poof!"

At the stop sign, Seth turned left. "Glenda doesn't know for sure that he was running from something. She just thinks he was."

"But we *know* he was." She heard the crack in her voice but was simply too tired to undo it or apologize for it. "Because of what he wrote."

"Running from something doesn't have to necessarily mean he did something awful."

She didn't mean to laugh nor could she help it. It was either that or cry. "He ran to keep from going to jail, Seth. People don't worry about going to jail unless they've done something wrong."

At the next stop sign, Seth hesitated for a few moments, his focus moving between the road and Penny. "Maybe that's not what he meant by steel bars. Maybe he came here just because he wanted a change of job or geography. It happens, you know."

"Oh, I know. It's why I'm here." She looked out at the passing trees, seeing none of them. "Going through my mother's things... Being in that house without her... It just got so heavy I felt like I was suffocating."

She didn't need to turn her head to know Seth pitied her. She could feel it filling the space between them just as surely as she could feel him change his right turn to a left turn. "But what my grandfather wrote? It was different. Desperate, almost. And he hid it. Under a floorboard. Why would he hide it if it wasn't something bad?"

"I don't know." It was a simple answer, void of any baseless platitudes, but for just a moment, she couldn't help but wish he'd said something else—something that could make the turmoil in her heart disappear. Instead, he made another turn, slowed the truck to a stop at the mouth of an unfamiliar driveway, and nudged his chin and her questioning eyes toward the view on the other side of the windshield.

Penny took a moment to study the attractive two-story log home. The colorful mums flanking the front walkway... The handful of rockers grouped together on the front porch that stretched from one end of the house to the other... The miniature, playhouse version of the same house beneath a large, stately oak tree...

It took a moment to find her words, another her voice. "Where are we?" she whispered.

Before Seth could answer, Rita stepped up from somewhere behind the truck and pulled open Penny's door with a mile-wide smile on her face. "I can't imagine a more wonderful sight than seeing the two of you here. Together."

"Mommmm."

"What?" Rita spread her arms wide. "Are you not both here? At the same time? In the same vehicle?"

"I repeat: Mommmm."

Waving a dismissive hand at her son and his protests, Rita beckoned Penny from the truck with her other. "Welcome, welcome. You caught me during a much-needed break from the store, and I couldn't be more pleased that you did. Come. Sit with me on the front porch. Tell me how you're doing with that project list of yours."

"I painted the kitchen last night," Penny said as she and Seth both exited the truck.

Rita clapped her hands, once, twice. "That's wonderful! How does it look?"

Penny opened her mouth to answer, but Seth beat her to it. "It looks great. That pale yellow you two picked out really lightened the room in a rather pleasing way."

"I knew it would!" Rita beckoned them to follow her onto the porch and then dispatched Seth inside to get them something to drink. While he did, Rita pointed Penny to the rocking chair in the center of the cluster. "Is my very handsome and incredibly kind-hearted son making himself useful, sweetheart?"

It was hard not to smile at the blatant hope in the woman's face. It was even harder to keep from laughing at Seth's eye roll as he returned to the porch in time to hear his mother's question. "He's been amazing, actually," Penny said, honestly.

"He cooks too! Quite well, actually!"

Seth handed Penny a glass of iced tea and set one down on the table next to his mother. "Mom, please."

"What? Do you not cook? Do you not do your own laundry? Do you not keep the cleanest house of any man I've ever known?"

Before Seth could follow up yet another eye roll with a pointed reprimand, Penny jumped in. "Trust me, I know. His blueberry muffins? They were mind-blowing."

Rita's eyes lit up like a Christmas tree as she looked from Penny to Seth and back again. "He made you his special muffins?"

"I figured her food options are limited, seeing as how she just got here." Seth palmed his face. Shook his head. Dropped his hand to the armrest of his rocking chair with a thud. "Anyway, I thought maybe you could share a memory of Penny's grandfather with her, since you were classmates with her mom and all."

"Oh Seth, Kate and I were far more than just classmates. We were inseparable. In school and out. If I wasn't at her house, she was at mine."

Penny stilled her glass halfway to her mouth. "So, you spent real time around my grandfather?"

Rita smiled. "I did."

"What was he like?" she asked, lowering her glass back down to her lap.

"He and your grandmother were always so kind and welcoming. Your grandma was always making us cookies, and your grandpa was always coming up with some sort of fun thing we could do." Rita took a sip from her glass as she seemed to travel to a different time and place. "Your grandfather wasn't like the other adults I knew."

Seth's rocker creaked to a stop. "How so?"

"Most adults were always telling us things—how to do something, how not to do something, what to do, what not to do, et cetera. But your grandfather, Penny? He was always asking us questions."

"What kind of questions?" Penny asked in unison with Seth.

"He'd ask us what we thought about things, what we wanted to do or be, what made us happy, that sort of stuff. And when we'd answer, he'd listen." Rita looked out at her front yard even though it was clear she wasn't really seeing it. "That always stuck out to me. Even then. Because it was…different. Most adults didn't listen to what we kids had to say about important stuff."

Seth stood, wandered over to the railing, turned, and leaned against it. "You're like that, Mom. Always have been. With all of us, even the grandkids."

"If I am, it's because Penny's grandfather showed me how important it is to a person's self-worth to be asked for their thoughts, their ideas, their dreams, their feelings."

Penny pondered the woman's words for a few moments, silently comparing them to everything she'd heard about the man while growing up. They all fit. But—

"Mrs. Farmer felt he was running from something when he came to Deadwood," Penny said.

Rita stared at her. "I didn't know Glenda was leaving her house anymore. I understood her live-in caregiver ran all her outside errands."

"I took Penny *to* her," Seth volunteered. "Just before we came here."

Again, Rita looked from Seth to Penny and back, her eyebrows as much a giveaway to her surprise as her tone. "Why would you do that?"

"Seth thought she might be able to shed a little light on my grandfather as he was when he first came to Deadwood."

"And Glenda felt he was running from something?" Rita asked.

Seth nodded along with Penny's *yes*.

"Why would she say that?"

"Because when she asked him about where he came from, he wouldn't tell her."

"Roland was the foreman at the lumber mill who hired him," Seth said, glancing at Penny. "And Glenda described Penny's grandfather as being sullen."

Rita waved the notion away as if it were a pesky gnat. "Maybe he was feeling ill that day. Or maybe he simply woke up on the wrong side of the bed. But whatever the case, the man *I* knew was anything but sullen."

"It wasn't just one encounter," Penny said. "Mrs. Farmer said he continuously dodged her questions about his life before Deadwood."

"So?" Rita countered, not unkindly. "Maybe he didn't feel like talking about it when she asked him. Or maybe he'd gotten wind that Glenda, while mostly harmless, has always been drawn to gossip—hearing it and spreading it."

For a split second, Penny felt her spirits lift at the possibility that Glenda's hypothesizing was just that, hypothesizing. But it didn't last. Because as much as she wanted to discount the centenarian's words, she had her grandfather's.

"Did he ever tell *you* about his life before Deadwood?" Penny asked.

"No, not that I recall. At least not in plain language."

Seth frowned. "Meaning?"

"He asked me once what I wanted to be when I grew up. I told him I wanted to be a mom and I wanted to own a store."

"Well, you certainly did that," Seth mused.

"I did." Rita took another sip of her tea. "But what I remember most about that conversation all those years ago is his response. He didn't tell me I should just be a teacher or a nurse as was more the expectation for women back then. Instead, he told me I should go home that very day and tell my parents what I wanted to do. He told me I should tell them and show them every single day."

Penny toed her own rocker to a stop. "Show them? Show them how?"

Rita's soft laughter filled the porch. "Your mom and I played store every time we were at my house after that. Clothes store. Grocery store. And, yes, on occasion, even hardware store. Needless to say, when Kate went off to college and I stayed behind to work at the store Seth's father and I bought after our marriage, no one in my family was the least bit surprised."

It was a fun thing to hear, but it did nothing to help quiet the nagging questions in her heart. Instead, Penny placed her still-full glass onto a nearby table and stood. "This has been a lovely visit, Rita, but I really should be going. I have a list of tasks to complete that's nearly as long as my arm, and my window of time in which to do them is growing shorter every day."

Rita peeked at her watch, grunted, and reluctantly stood as well. "And I should be getting back to the store before Seth's father sends out a search party."

Pushing off the railing, Seth followed Penny over to the steps. "I'll drop Penny off and meet you at the store in twenty."

"No. Stay and help Penny at the house." Rita gathered up the glasses. "If anyone comes in requesting a delivery, I'll text you. Otherwise, Dad and I can handle things just fine on our own."

Seth laughed. "Gee, thanks. You make me sound so... expendable."

"Not expendable, dear, I just—"

"Mom. Stop. Please."

"What? I didn't say anything wrong."

"You were about to."

Rita's answering huff held no sign of denial. The smile that followed showed only guilt.

"I can handle everything on my list," Penny protested. "Honest."

"I'm sure you can, dear. But my son will help you anyway."

Penny turned to the man holding her truck door open. "Seth, I don't need you to spend all your time helping—"

"Arguing with my mother is an exercise in futility. Trust me on this."

"But—"

"It's okay, Penny. I promise." He closed the door behind her and then rounded the truck to his spot behind the steering wheel. "Besides, helping fix up a place my mom hung out in as a kid is proving to be kind of fun."

She fastened her seat belt and waved goodbye to Rita as Seth backed out of the driveway. "Hmm... I think there's another reason you're going along with this forced helping stuff."

"You mean besides the fact I'm afraid of my mother?" he joked.

"Yup."

Clearing his throat, he shifted in his seat, waiting.

"Based on the way your cheeks are turning red, I'm right, aren't I?" Penny blew out a breath as she turned her attention to the road in front of them. "But really, I don't want to be one of only two people our age in a town where everyone has someone. It'll just make the loneliness worse. Renting the house out is the only thing that makes sense. So, if the reason you're helping has anything to do with trying to convince me not to, please don't. My plate can't handle anything else right now."

CHAPTER NINE

Slowly but surely, they worked their way down her list for the hallway and the bedroom, Seth repairing or replacing floorboards and Penny prepping and priming the walls for painting. After their single, near collision, they course-corrected and soon settled into a routine that afforded them the space they both needed. Most of the time they worked in companiable silence, each intent on their own task, their own thoughts. But sometimes, when a song came over Seth's phone that they both liked, it served as a much-needed break from the proverbial tooth Penny kept wiggling in her mind.

Oh, how she wanted to believe Rita was right, that Glenda's comments about Grandpa Jon were nothing more than the churnings of a lifelong gossip. But every time she got herself to a point where she almost could, the memory of his journal entry forced itself to the forefront of her mind.

"Grip that primer brush any harder, and it just might split in two."

A glance down at her hand and its whitening knuckles showed the truth in Seth's words. "I wasn't aware," she said, forcing herself to relax.

"That's because you've been somewhere other than here for the past ten minutes or so." Seth slid the hammer through a loop in his tool belt and stood. "You okay?"

She dipped the end of her brush into the can of primer and worked it across the wall closest to the door. "Help me get out of my own head for a little while, and I will be."

"Sure thing." Seth crossed to the far corner of the room and ran his hand along the window's edge. "What would you like to talk about?"

"Tell me about that playhouse next to your mom's house. It's an exact replica of the main house, only child-sized."

Reaching inside another pocket of his tool belt, Seth pulled out a piece of sandpaper and moved it back and forth against the edge of the wooden pane. "I made that two Christmases ago for my nieces and nephew."

Penny stilled her primer brush midstroke. "You made that?"

"I did."

"How did you learn to do that?"

He shrugged. "A lot of trial and error, mostly. But somehow it all came together pretty well."

"It sure did." She added more primer to her brush and continued down the wall. "And your nieces and nephew? Were they thrilled?"

"After I showed it to them, they didn't come out for close to an hour. In the dead of winter."

"At least you know they liked it." When she reached the end of the wall, she stepped back, surveyed her work, and gave her arms and shoulders a much-needed stretch. "For my third birthday, my mom and dad set up a makeshift restaurant in my playroom. They made a pair of menus with pictures of the plastic food items I had, my dad made a little table that fit me and my dolls, and my mom made a red-and-white tablecloth and an apron that said,

'Penny's Place' across the front. I think I played restaurant at some point every day after that for the next two years."

"Do you remember much about your dad, seeing as how you were only four when he died?"

"Not as much as I wish I did. Sometimes I have flashes of memory, but I don't always know if they're mine or ones I heard my mom talk about as I was growing up."

"I imagine that had to be mighty hard on your mom, especially with you being so little."

Backtracking to a spot on the wall she'd clearly done during one of her more distracted moments, she added a few brushstrokes of primer. "I'm sure it was. But somehow she carried on, determined to give me the best childhood possible. And she did."

Seth ran his fingers across the area he'd sanded and, when he deemed it acceptable, shoved the sandpaper into his pocket. "My mom says you're the spitting image of your mother."

"I wish." Penny tapped the primer can closed with the handle of the flathead screwdriver she'd used to open it, set her brush down on top of it, and hooked her thumb toward the door. "Would you like to see a picture?"

"Absolutely."

Pleased, Penny led the way into the living room. A quick glance around yielded the location of her purse and, inside it, the wallet-sized photograph she carried of her mom. She took a moment to drink in the face she desperately missed and then handed it to Seth. "My mother, Katherine McCormick. The way I will always remember her *before* she got sick. Happy and so full of life."

"And beautiful," he added, looking at the picture.

"Inside *and* out."

"Wow. My mom wasn't kidding, was she? It's like looking at you twenty years from now. The same cheeks, the same curve to the chin, and even the same smile save for the way it stops short of your eyes."

Penny breathed through the answering tightness in her throat. "If my smile doesn't reach my eyes, it's because I lost *her*."

Seth took one last look at the picture and then handed it back to Penny, his anguish over her loss palpable. "Do you have any other pictures of your family? Maybe of you and your mom together, or both of you with your dad when you were little? Because I'd love to see them if you do."

"I do but not here." She drew the picture to her heart. "They're all at my place in Tennessee in—wait! That's not true. I actually have one of my Grandpa Jon too. It was inside the book we found the other day."

With one last glance at her mom, Penny tucked the picture inside her purse and crossed to the coffee table and the book that both drew her and repelled her with equal measure. She flipped past the poems and the thoughtful ponderings about life until she reached the black-and-white photograph of the man she knew only from stories.

"We had a picture, almost exactly like this one, on our mantel when I was growing up." She handed the photograph to Seth, studying it with him across the top of his arm.

"He didn't have a sister, did he?" Seth asked.

"No, why?"

"His scar looks a lot like mine." Seth pointed to a thin line above his left eyebrow. "Only mine was thanks to my sister and a fast-moving doorknob."

Penny mouthed an *ouch* and then directed Seth's attention back to the photo. "In the picture I grew up with, he was sitting, deep in thought, like I imagine he might've looked while writing about something that had touched his soul."

Seth held the picture out, tilting it left to right. "Yet, in this one, he looks like he's—I don't know. The antithesis of deep thought, I guess?"

"I think he looks a little smug," Penny said. "Like it's all about him."

"Yeah, I can see that."

"Which is interesting. Because Grandpa Jon, as I was raised to think of him, fit with the picture on our mantel. Grandpa Jon as he may have *actually* been, might go better with this one."

Seth returned the print to Penny. "I hate that you have to have this uncertainty on top of everything else you've gone through."

"You and me both." She took one last look at the picture and then retrieved the still-open book from its spot on the coffee table. "The only silver lining—if there's one to be had—is that my mom didn't have to have it too."

She replaced the picture between the pages and closed the book, her gaze finding and then mentally tracing the name embossed in gold lettering across the bottom edge of the cover. "It's weird to think that the name my mother had throughout her entire childhood may have been made up, shortened down from—wait! That's it!"

"What's it?" Seth asked.

"I know his real name. I know where he came from before Deadwood. And"—she flipped back the cover to reveal a mother's dated letter to her son—"I have a general time frame as to when he most likely left Chicago."

"You have a computer?" Seth asked.

She felt her body deflate. "I do. But there's no Wi-Fi, and my hot spot only seems to work in the morning, if at all."

"That's okay. I've got decent Wi-Fi at my place you're welcome to use."

"When?"

"Well, the primer needs to dry before we can paint, so how about now?"

It took some fiddling with the date, but, eventually, they got a hit. It was little more than a mention in a piece about 1950s Chicago, but it was akin to striking gold in the moment.

In it, a Jonathan Devonshire from the south side of Chicago was mentioned as standing in for his father, Richard Devonshire, President of Devonshire Homes, at a meeting with city officials.

"It would make sense that it's him," Seth mused from his spot just over Penny's left shoulder.

Penny read the blurb again. "Why do you say that?"

"His work at Deadwood Lumber and how he built your house himself." Seth blew out a breath. "The job, on its own, could've just been about taking what he could get. But building the house the way he did? That speaks to experience."

It made sense.

She flipped open her grandfather's book and stared down at her great-grandmother's inscription.

I also know that to deny your ability as a carpenter will only spite yourself. Don't do that. You took to your father's world like a duck to water. That's not a judgment or a statement made to induce guilt, but, rather, a simple truth. Still, I hope you will always find a way to let your ability with pen and paper be a part of your life, as it's as much a part of you as your soul.

Let this be the place where you allow yourself to nurture that gift while making your own way in this world. Never, ever, forget how much I love you and how endlessly blessed I've been to be your mother.

"I think you're right. See?" She held the page out for Seth to read. "His mother actually references his carpentry ability in her inscription."

"And if he's the same Jonathan Devonshire we just found, his father owning a company bearing the Devonshire name would certainly work with the line she wrote right after that."

Tilting the book in such a way that she too could see it, she returned her attention to the top of the inscription and read it again, this time aloud.

There are no words for the pain I feel over your decision to leave Chicago, but I understand. Anyone who doesn't value the generous and kindhearted young man you are doesn't deserve to walk this life with you no matter who they are or how right they may seem on the surface.

She stopped and considered what she'd read. "Maybe he had a fight with his father? And that's what he ran from?" she posed.

Seth gave a half nod, half shrug. "Maybe. But if you take that in conjunction with the next paragraph, it seems as if she might be referencing more of a romantic relationship."

Penny's gaze followed Seth's finger to the next few lines.

You are deserving of someone who sees and knows you for who you truly are. And I know that one day, when the time is right, you will find that person. Of that, I have no doubt. When you do, please be yourself. Show her the man I know you to be, the one you've always been for anyone who cared to see beyond the matching exterior.

"The matching exterior part is strange, but maybe he ran from a broken heart?" she suggested, looking up. "Maybe from someone who chose him based on looks alone?"

Another half nod, half shrug. "It's possible," Seth said before taking over the duty of reading the last two paragraphs aloud, once again.

I also know that to deny your ability as a carpenter will only spite yourself. Don't do that. You took to your father's world like a duck to water. That's not a judgment or a statement made to induce guilt, but, rather, a simple truth. Still, I hope you will always find a way to let your ability with pen and paper be a part of your life, as it's as much a part of you as your soul.

Let this book be the place where you allow yourself to nurture that gift while making your own way in this world. Never, ever, forget how much I love you and how endlessly blessed I've been to be your mother.

"Do you get the sense that maybe Grandpa Jon's father wanted him to be a carpenter and Grandpa Jon wanted to be a writer?" Penny felt a headache brewing and did her best to knead it away.

"That's my guess," Seth mused.

"If not for the part about running to avoid jail time, I'd find his choice to come here, to a place like Deadwood, odd. I mean, why travel so far to work in a lumber mill when you could stay in Chicago and do the same thing for your father—with the perks that surely came with being the owner's son?"

Seth stood. Stretched. "To make it on his own? In his own right? I mean, I know *I* can certainly understand that. Fortunately, I don't have to go halfway across the country and change my name in order to make my own life. My parents support me and my decisions."

She couldn't help but smile even it if was fleeting. "Your mom sure seems keen on you not remaining single."

"True. But if that's what I really wanted, she wouldn't push." Seth motioned toward the door of his study. "Hey, I don't know about you, but I'm starving. Let me make us some dinner before it's time to get you back to your house."

She closed her laptop and rose to her feet. "I've taken way too much of your time already today as it is. You absolutely do not have to make me dinner."

"I know I don't, but I want to. Case closed."

Chapter Ten

Dinner was, in a word, delicious. The steaks were grilled to perfection, the baked potatoes soft on the inside and crispy on the outside, and the dressing on the spinach salad was both sweet and tangy. And while there were occasional lulls in the conversation during various parts of the meal, it was okay. Because there was something very calming about being in Seth's house.

The furnishings leaned toward dark colors the way men tended to choose, but there was a distinct flair of homeyness too, in everything from the pot holders his eldest niece had made him to the pair of sippy cups that sat alongside regular drinking glasses in the cabinet next to the sink.

In the small yet cozy living room where they retired to digest after dinner, the simple wooden mantel gracing his fireplace was covered in pictures—some with Seth, some without, but all of them family.

And the overstuffed couch that felt like a giant bear hug on her tired and achy body the second she sat down? No words. None.

"I run or ride my bike nearly every day at home, yet just about every muscle in my body seems to be screaming at me right now." Penny pulled a nearby throw pillow onto her lap and watched the log Seth lit flame to life. "Every. Single. One."

Seth closed the fireplace screen and made his way over to the couch, claiming a spot a few feet from Penny. "On the surface, stuff like painting and cleaning and fixing floors doesn't look like it'd be exercise. But a few hours later, when your arms hurt from all those brushstrokes and your thighs and back hurt from all that bending and squatting, you get set straight."

"You don't seem to be hurting."

"That's because I do this kind of stuff all the time. My muscles are used to it." Seth crossed his legs and let out a sigh. "But bike or run every day like you just said? Trust me, I'd be feeling *that* just as much as you're feeling this stuff."

She watched the flames reach hungrily toward the chimney and allowed herself a moment to say nothing, think nothing, do nothing. Instead, she lost herself in the crackling and hissing of the firewood.

"So how are you feeling about this stuff with your grandfather?" Seth stretched his arm across the back of the couch only to remove it as his fingertips brushed against Penny's neck.

Resting her left cheek against the couch, she was surprised but not unpleased to find Seth's gaze waiting for hers. "One minute, I want answers. The next, I don't. It's hard."

"Do you have any family left?" Seth asked. "Aunts? Uncles? Cousins? Anyone?"

"My mom and my dad were both only children. So I'm the last of the line." She popped up her head and pointed his attention toward the mantel. "What you have? With your parents? With your siblings and their families? I can't even imagine what that would be like."

Seth turned so his body was flush with the armrest and his view was squarely on Penny. "Do you ever wish you'd had a sibling?"

"When my mom first passed—of course. I desperately wished there was someone I could call, someone who would understand my pain and not try to pat it away. Still do, sometimes. But in order to change that, the rest of my life with my mother would have to have been different. And I wouldn't change one single iota about our time together. Not a one."

"Tell me about her."

For a moment she didn't think she could. Just the idea of it made her eyes sting and her throat tighten. But when she looked at the pictures lined up along the mantel and thought about the stories they told, she found herself wanting to talk, to help someone else see the amazing gift her mother had been in her life. "She was... *everything.* Kind. Generous. Loving. She believed wholeheartedly that her life was a gift from God and that living it well and raising me right was her gift to Him.

"When we were together, she was completely present. At the dinner table, on a trip, when she was helping me with homework, when we sat on the back porch together, and even in those last few months when the cancer made it so she was too weak to leave her bed. I never had to compete for her attention with a computer or a phone. I never doubted my importance in her life. I never, ever, doubted her love for me."

Now that she was talking, she found she couldn't stop. "My mom taught me how to cook and bake, and I taught her how to line dance. She showed me the difference between a good book and a great book. She believed in always being open to new friends. She treated friends like family. She taught me the importance of creativity in solving problems and never batted so much as an eyelash when I said I wanted to find a way to write for a living. The fact that I wanted to do it and had my heart set on it was enough for her to champion me. And…"

She squeezed her eyes closed. Swallowed. Shook her head.

"And what?" Seth prompted.

Penny swallowed again. Opened her eyes. "I miss her so much, Seth. I miss her every second of every minute. Every minute of every hour. Every hour of every day."

"I can see why."

She tried to keep her tears in check, but when Seth took her into his arms, she began to sob—gut-wrenching sobs that started deep inside her heart and continued until she was too tired to cry another tear. Finally, she pulled back, tried to wipe away the wetness from his flannelled shoulder, and collapsed against the couch, spent. "I bet you're wishing you'd never offered up your Wi-Fi," she said on the heels of a hiccup.

"Not at all." He paused as if he was going to say something else, but he simply tucked a dampened strand of hair behind her ear instead. "You can use my Wi-Fi anytime you want."

She mustered the smile his kindness warranted and then scooted off the couch and onto her feet. "You should probably take me back to the house now. Morning will be here before we know it. When it comes, I have a room to paint and you have breakfast with your family."

"You could push the painting off until the afternoon and come have pancakes and bacon at my mom and dad's place."

"Thank you for the offer, but I'm not going to crash your family's Sunday morning tradition."

He stood. "It's not crashing if you're invited. And I'm inviting you."

"I—"

"I'll be the first to admit my family can be a lot sometimes. And if you're there, my siblings will have a field day trying to one-up each other in who can tell the most embarrassing stories about me. But when I head home after spending time with them, I always feel lighter no matter what may or may not have been bothering me when I got there."

She looked from Seth to the pictures on the mantel, the sincerity of his invite coupled with the intensity of his gaze impossible to miss. "Being with my mom always did the same for me."

"Then come. Meet my family. Witness how they make sure I will never have a swollen ego. Eat some pancakes. Come to church with us beforehand if you'd like. And then, when you give me the high sign, I'll get you out of there so you can go home."

"And you don't think your mom will read into that?" Penny asked.

"Oh, she'll absolutely read into it," Seth said, grinning. "This *is* my mom we're talking about. But trust me, I can handle it."

Seth was right. His mother's pancakes were delicious. Every member of his family had not only welcomed Penny to their weekly ritual but also managed to make her feel like she belonged. His siblings did, in fact, enjoy sharing the kinds of stories that made adult Seth squirm— and turn five shades of red in the process. And Rita didn't even try to hide her pleasure over Seth having invited Penny to brunch.

In the moment it had been exactly what Penny needed—fun and uplifting. But afterward, on her drive back to the house, fun and uplifting bowed to a near soul-crushing sadness. No, she'd never had thirteen people around a table for a Sunday morning brunch the way Seth did each week, but she'd lived that kind of warmth and belonging and known that same kind of unconditional love with her mom. She knew its power. Knew its gravity.

And now, it was just...*gone*.

Seth had been surrounded by people who knew everything about him. His parents remembered his birth, his older sisters remembered carting him around like a doll, his brother remembered catching frogs in the river with him, and his nieces and nephew looked at him like he was something special. Everyone at that table knew Seth inside and out, just as he knew all of them. There was no one left in Penny's life who knew her when she was born, no one who heard her utter her first word or saw her take her first step, or knew her the way Seth and his family clearly knew one another. Everyone who knew her was gone. Except Penny.

And all Penny had left of her family was stories and memories and—

"A great big old question mark about Grandpa Jon," she murmured as she turned left at the end of Rita's road and continued west toward the house.

Road by road, Penny made her way to the family homestead her mother had been so anxious for her to visit. *That house was where your grandparents fell in love, Penny... The house always brought me such peace, Penny... Go there, remember the stories I've always told you, and feel me the way my stories helped you feel them...*

"I'm here, Mom," she whispered. "And I'm trying. I really am. I'm learning stuff I don't think you knew. Like maybe the reason you could never finish Grandpa Jon's side of the family tree was because his real last name was Devonshire, not Devons. Maybe if you'd known that, you'd have found—"

She veered onto the road's overgrown shoulder and rested her head against the seat. Was it possible? Might she still have some family left after all? It was a serious thought, one that both calmed and unsettled her in equal parts before intrigue trumped them both and sent her on her way. Only instead of continuing on to the house, she did a U-turn and headed back to town and the coffee shop she prayed had good Wi-Fi.

CHAPTER ELEVEN

Reaching underneath the pages of notes she'd lined up across her grandfather's coffee table, Penny felt around until she found the source of the on-again, off-again vibration. A quick check of the phone's illuminated screen and the name displayed across it had her hitting the green button.

"Hey, Seth. Thanks again for this morning. Your family is really pretty great."

"They all think you're pretty great too." He paused then cleared his throat. "Any chance you're still painting?"

She wedged the phone between her shoulder and her ear and continued sifting through the notes she'd made at the coffee shop. "Actually, I just got home about ten minutes ago."

"Did you go by way of Siberia?" he teased.

"Ha ha. More like by way of the coffee shop."

"If you'd told me you wanted another cup of coffee, I'd have made you one."

She skimmed her way across each piece of paper, stopping when she reached the name and number she sought. "I didn't go for the coffee. Just the internet."

"If you'd told me you wanted to use your computer, you could've used it at my mom's or gone back to my place with me."

"I didn't know I was going to use it until after I left. But Seth, I found something—something big. About my grandfather."

A noise indicative of Seth standing, or perhaps sitting if he'd been standing to start with, was quick, fleeting. "I'm listening."

"First, my great-grandmother—the one who wrote that inscription in Grandpa Jon's book—passed away not more than a year after Grandpa Jon left Chicago. Seems she died following a relatively quick illness, and her husband, Richard—Grandpa Jon's father—remarried less than six months later."

"That's fast," Seth mused.

"I thought so too, but to each his own, I guess." Penny pulled the page bearing the best part of the story onto her lap. "Anyway, a few years after *that*, Devonshire Homes closed up shop for good."

"Did whatever you read in your research say why it closed?"

"No. But in wandering down one rabbit hole after the next, I came across the name of my great-grandfather's second wife and… guess what?"

"She's still alive?"

Penny turned phone-holding duty back over to her hand. "She's not, but her daughter, Audrey, is! And I'm sitting here, right now, looking at not only her name but her phone number too."

"Wow," Seth said. "Nice detective work."

She gave into the grin stirred by his words. "Thank you."

"So? Are you going to call her?"

Penny looked again at the name and the number and allowed herself a long, slow breath. "I think I am. Now, in fact. I mean, I know we're not related by blood, but—"

"No buts, Penny. If this woman can help quiet your questions about your grandfather once and for all, it's worth a try, right?"

"*I* think it is."

"Then I'll let you go so you can make that call," he said. "But if you want to talk when you're done or decide to get back to painting and would like some help, give me a call."

"Thanks, Seth."

When a quick check of the phone screen confirmed their call had ended, Penny punched in the number she'd written and held her breath as it began to ring.

One ring…

Two rings…

Three—

"Compton residence, this is Milly."

"Hi. I was hoping to speak with"—Penny looked at the paper clutched in her hand—"Audrey?"

Milly's voice grew muffled. "I don't know what you're selling, but you need to quit calling folks on the weekend. It's disgraceful."

"I'm not selling anything. My name is Penny McCormick. Can you tell me if Audrey Compton was related in any way to a Richard Devonshire?"

"Her mother was married to Richard Devonshire."

Powered by a rush of nervous energy, Penny stood. "Could I speak with her, please?"

"If you're looking for money, Ms. McCormick, there's none to be had."

Penny wandered over to the window and rested her forehead against the cool glass. "I'm not looking for money. I promise. I'm just looking for… I don't know, exactly. Maybe some answers. Maybe just a chance to talk to someone who knew him."

She could hear Milly breathing, assessing, weighing, on the other end of the phone. But just as Penny began to worry whether the woman was going to deny her request, Milly spoke again. "Mrs. Compton is easily confused most days. Don't know what she's going to say from one minute to the next. Sometimes she makes sense, but most times she doesn't. But since she's having a relatively good day today, you're welcome to try if you'd like."

Before Penny could thank Milly, another voice—this one shaky and difficult to discern—came on the phone. "You knew my stepfather?"

"Technically, no, but I'm the—"

"How did you find me?"

"I found your name while doing a little research into Richard Devonshire and his company, Devonshire Homes."

A string of garbled sounds, followed by Milly's muffled voice in the background, ended as quickly as it had come. "My stepfather was a very weak man."

Penny pulled away from the window. "Excuse me?"

"Not at first." Audrey's cough was loud, long, and deep. "At first, he was wonderful. Driven, as my mother always said. He wanted the Devonshire name to be known. When they first got married, there were always parties at the house. The kind of affairs with fancy dresses and important people. Everyone in Chicago wanted to know him. But then it all just went away."

"What went away?" Penny asked.

"Everything that mattered."

Penny looked out at the trees her mother had once climbed and tried to make sense of what she was hearing. When she came up empty, she moved the conversation further down the line. "Why did Richard decide to close Devonshire Homes? Do you know?"

"He had no choice. He didn't realize the money was gone until it was too late."

"What money?" Penny asked, her voice shaky.

"The money in the company's reserve accounts. All of it. Except the bare minimum needed to keep them open."

Penny stared up at the ceiling. Swallowed.

"Should've gone to jail if you ask me," Audrey hissed.

She squeezed her eyes closed. Swallowed again.

"Good-for-nothings is what they were."

"Who?" Penny asked, despite knowing it was a rhetorical question.

"His blood."

"Do you mean his *son*, Jonathan?"

A string of garbled words Penny couldn't quite decipher carried on for a few minutes until, like a momentary burst of sun on an otherwise cloudy day, Audrey's voice grew clear once again. "Good riddance, I say. To both."

Before Penny could fully process the elderly woman's words, the line went dead. A second call to the same number simply rang and rang, unanswered.

"What on earth?" she mumbled as, again, she dialed the number and, again, it rang and rang, unanswered.

Frustrated, Penny made her way back to the coffee table and the notes she'd made at the coffee shop. By her calculations, Audrey

Compton was somewhere in her eighties. Milly, the woman Penny suspected was Audrey's caretaker, had warned her the woman was easily confused. But even with some of the garbled rambling, her great-grandfather's stepdaughter had seemed to follow along with the conversation fairly well. Until the end.

Had she been saying good riddance to Penny? Or to Penny and her inquiries about Richard Devonshire?

Sinking onto the couch, Penny let out a long sigh. Somehow, someway, the call she'd made in the hopes of quieting her questions had only made things worse. Much, much worse.

CHAPTER TWELVE

The bell over the front door welcomed Penny to Foster's Hardware little more than thirty seconds before Rita's voice rang out from somewhere deep inside the store.

"Welcome to Foster's, I'll be right with you."

Penny knew she should identify herself so as to keep Seth's mother from rushing through a task, but she didn't. She'd purposely waited outside in the parking lot for nearly twenty minutes until all visible customers had vacated the building. The last thing she wanted was for another one to walk in before she had a chance to talk to Rita alone.

Walking briskly, she surveyed the first three aisles and was approaching the fourth when Rita stepped out of the fifth and came to a halt, the corners of her generous mouth drawing upward in a heartfelt smile. "Oh! Penny! Hello!" Rita wiped her hands down the front of her apron and, on closer inspection of Penny, hastily closed the gap between them. "Is everything okay, dear? You don't look well."

Penny tried to speak but, instead, just shook her head lest she burst into tears right there in the middle of the hardware store.

"Oh Penny... Come. Come with me into the back where we can talk." Rita looked around, set the stack of washers she'd been holding on a nearby shelf, and pressed a small button on a tiny microphone dangling from around her neck. "Seth, I'm stepping into my office for a little bit, and I need you to cover inside the shop until I'm done."

Then Rita beckoned Penny to follow her past the customer service counter and into a small, windowless office. When they were safely inside, Rita shut the door and gathered Penny's hands inside her own. "What's going on, sweetheart? You look like you've been up all night."

Penny nodded, once, twice. Kneaded at the growing ache in her left temple. "He wasn't what you or I thought he was. Wasn't what"—she sucked in a breath, steadied her voice—"Mom thought either. And that's the part that kills me most. Though… I don't know.… Maybe the fact that she doesn't have to know this is a blessing?"

She shook off the chair Rita offered and looked down at her feet in an effort to stifle a strangled cry. "You know, so she could leave this earth believing the fantasy?"

"What fantasy, Penny?"

"The one that had my grandpa Jon being some sort of pillar of society. A veritable paragon of integrity and compassion and all the other bogus traits he knowingly and erroneously allowed people to equate him with."

Rita drew back so fast she bumped into the room's metal desk, nearly toppling a stack of papers to the floor. "Good heavens, Penny, what are you talking about?"

"My grandfather. Jonathan Devons. Or *Jonathan Devonshire* if you happened to have known him in his Chicago days."

"Jonathan Devonshire?" Rita repeated.

Penny nodded. Swallowed. Nodded again.

"I never heard him referred to as that."

"That's because he didn't want anyone to know him by that name." Leaning back against the wall, Penny met, held, and then released Rita's skepticism with a labored sigh. "And with very good reason, I might add."

Rita haphazardly restacked the papers, shoved them to the middle of the desk, and then perched on its edge. "Since I have absolutely no idea where you're going with this, I need you to take it from the top."

"My grandfather's real name was Jonathan Devonshire. He came to Deadwood all those years ago because he was on the run." The same chill she'd been experiencing off and on since she first spoke to Audrey Compton the previous evening made its way up her spine once again. Only this time, instead of being the result of growing uncertainty, it was about dread and sadness and a truth she couldn't pretend away no matter how much she wished she could. "He rightly figured that a place the size of Deadwood, Oregon, would be the perfect place to hide from what he'd done. And changing his name? That just made it even easier to fool people. Like my grandmother into marrying him… Like my mom who all but worshipped him… Like the people in this town who you say thought the world of him… And even me, who never met him, yet fell for all the same stories that were handed down to me my whole life."

When it became clear Rita was holding any and all comments until she'd heard everything, Penny continued, her voice vacillating between anger and sadness on an almost second-to-second basis. "But he wasn't that person. He was a cheat and a thief and—"

"A cheat and a thief?" Rita echoed. "Jonathan Devons?"

"Jonathan *Devonshire*," Penny corrected. "And if he hadn't run, he'd have gone to jail. Which is where he belonged."

Rita gripped the edge of the desk and slowly shook her head. "Penny, I don't know where you got this, but it has to be wrong. It has to be."

Penny's smile was powered by something much different than joy. "I thought that too. Until I simply couldn't anymore."

"I don't understand."

"My grandfather's dad—my great-grandfather, Richard Devonshire—owned a construction company in Chicago called Devonshire Homes. It was wildly successful for its time. The kind of business that afforded Richard and Vivian—my great-grandmother—and, when she died, Richard's new wife, Rose, and her daughter, Audrey, a fairly affluent lifestyle. From what I was able to gather during my research in the wee hours of the night, they were true who's who types in Chicago at that time.

"When my grandfather left Chicago, everyone—including his mother, Vivian—believed it was due to a broken engagement."

Rita frowned. "Jon was engaged to someone before Roberta?"

"I don't know her name or anything about her, as I didn't want to waste my limited research window on what clearly wasn't the main motivation in him coming here, but yes. He was."

"Wow. I had no idea."

Penny parted company with the wall and began wandering around the tiny room—from wall to desk, from desk to shop door, from shop door to filing cabinet, from filing cabinet to a door along the opposite wall, and then back again. "Anyway, it seems everyone thought that's why he left. That and, perhaps, to pursue his own career interests rather than taking over Devonshire Homes the way his father expected him to."

"But your grandfather worked at a lumber mill here. Built the house that's now yours. Made furniture on occasion."

Again, Penny nodded. "I was curious about that too. Why leave a company you were slated to take over in the future only to do the same basic work in a place where you were, essentially, nobody? I mean, if he'd made a go of the writing career his mother seemed to think he wanted, that part of the story would make sense, but there's nothing to indicate he did that from what I can see."

"Maybe he intended to, dear. But marriage and, eventually, a child, probably changed things for him," Rita offered. "Supporting a family as a writer—especially around here—just didn't happen then."

"Agreed. Which is why I circled back to the question, *why Deadwood*? A teeny tiny town, in the middle of nowhere, wasn't a place to go if you wanted to try your hand at a new profession."

"You mentioned the broken engagement," Rita reminded her. "Maybe that actually was the reason he left."

"No, I'm quite sure the real reason was something very different. Something that would make a person run to avoid jail."

"Jail?" Rita echoed.

"Which is where he belonged after stealing from his father's company."

"Penny, you can't really believe that," Rita said on the heels of a gasp.

"I do after speaking to Richard's stepdaughter."

Rita stared at Penny. "Your great-grandfather's stepdaughter?"

"Yes."

"She's still alive?"

"She is. Although she suffers from some sort of dementia-related illness and is easily confused."

"Yet you think she's clear on this?" Rita asked.

"Yes," Penny said. "When coupled with tweaking his name and what he wrote in his journal? Absolutely."

For several minutes, Rita said nothing. She just looked at Penny as if she was waiting for a *gotcha*, or an *only kidding*. When it didn't come, Rita pushed off her desk and met Penny by the filing cabinet, understanding finally showing its head behind her initial shock and denial. "Even if this is true, Penny, this holds no reflection on you or your mom. Please tell me you know that."

"My head knows that," Penny whispered. "But all I have left of my family is the stories I was told about my grandparents, the stories I was told about my dad, and the memories Mom and I made. Finding out that some of those stories weren't true is—"

She heard the crack in her voice, felt the tremble in her lips, and willed herself not to cry again. "I'm not even sure why I came here, to your shop, except, I guess, because you knew her? Knew them?"

Rita cupped Penny's face between her hands. "Oh Penny, I know you're hurting, and I wish I could explain away all of this stuff you found. But it's news to me too. News that just doesn't fit with the man I remember."

Penny covered Rita's hands with her own and gently lowered them away from her face. "Apparently, Grandpa Jon was a gifted liar."

She saw Rita stiffen and likened it to the way she, herself, had felt at the mere notion her grandfather might've been something other than what she'd been told her whole life. If only she could go back to that place of naivete and denial.

"Did you sleep at all last night, Penny?"

"No."

"Then I want you to return to the house and get some sleep. This stuff about your grandfather will all be here when you wake up, unfortunately. But at least then you'll be better rested and can see it more clearly."

"I don't want to see it more clearly," Penny whispered.

"Meaning, with a clear head, you'll be able to see that none of this changes who you are or who your mom was. None of it."

She wanted to believe Rita was right. That the proverbial sins of the father didn't extend to her mom or to her, but it was hard. It felt like so much of what she'd relied on to shape her roots had been blown to smithereens in front of her face.

"I want to believe that. I really do."

"Then believe it, because it's true, Penny." Rita held her hand out. "Now come on, let me walk you to your car."

Penny looked from Rita to the still-closed door. "Is there a back door I could go out? I don't want to see anyone right now, if that's okay?"

Understanding lit Rita's warm brown eyes once again. "You don't want to see Seth?" she asked.

"I don't want to see anyone," Penny corrected. "I'm just not in the right headspace."

"I understand. And yes, you can exit straight into the parking lot from right here." Rita led Penny to a door and yanked it open to the late morning sunshine and the still empty parking lot beyond. "Put all of this out of your head for a little while and get some sleep, okay?"

Thirty minutes earlier, when she'd first walked into the hardware store, sleep was the last thing on Penny's mind. But now that she'd had a chance to share her findings and her worries aloud, it was as if the weight she'd been shouldering since the phone call with Audrey Compton had lessened enough that she might actually be able to sleep.

Stepping out into the crisp fall morning she'd barely noticed upon arrival, Penny yawned. "Thank you, Rita. I'll try."

CHAPTER THIRTEEN

She was staring at the ceiling over the couch when she heard the knock. And, for a moment, she actually considered feigning sleep and letting whoever it was give up and go away. But considering it was probably Rita coming to check on her, she knew she couldn't. Rita deserved better.

Glancing one last time at the picture she'd set on her stomach, she shifted it to the coffee table and made herself get up, walk down the hallway, and open the door to…Seth.

"Hey." She took in his boots, his khaki slacks and crisp white shirt, and tried not to compare it to her own jeans and paisley top, rumpled from the nap that never quite transpired. "I guess your mom told you about your toolbox?"

"My toolbox?" he asked. "No, why? What about it?"

"You left it here the other day."

"Oh yeah, I know. I knew I'd be back." He looked her over from head to toe, returning his full attention to hers in short order. "You okay? Mom told me about your call with your grandfather's stepsister."

She wanted to shrug the question off, to act as if none of it mattered, but to do that took a theatrical ability she knew she couldn't sell. "I know it shouldn't mean anything. I know it has nothing to do with me. But…" Penny leaned her shoulder against the open door. "I don't know."

"I do."

"You do?" She met his nod with a bitter-tinged laugh. "Yeah, I don't think so. You see your parents every day and your adult siblings and their families at least once a week. You know everything about them, and they know everything about you. Trust me, Seth, you most definitely don't know."

If her words stung, he didn't let on. Instead, he hooked his thumb toward his truck. "I'd like to take you somewhere for a little while if you're game."

Startled, she stared at him. "Take me where?"

"I'd rather let it speak for itself."

She looked past him to his truck then back at his attire and, finally, her own. "I'm really not feeling all that social."

"Give me thirty minutes, Penny. That's all."

It would be so easy to say no. The answer was on the tip of her tongue. But with everything he'd done to help around the house and the kindness he'd shown her over the past week, she could give him thirty minutes. Squaring her shoulders, she grabbed her keys, pulled the door shut, and followed him out to his truck for the short drive into town.

They passed his parents' hardware store.

They passed the coffee shop.

They passed the Deadwood Market.

They passed the ice cream shop.

And, just beyond the gas station, he pulled into a small lot and parked the truck next to a simple one-story building.

"Town hall?" She looked from the sign mounted above the building's front door to the man preparing to exit the truck. "Are we going to a wedding I don't know about?"

"Ha! The only wedding left to happen in this town would be my own. And trust me when I say there won't be a person in town my mom won't have told when that day comes."

She allowed herself the genuine smile at the truth in his words and followed him out of the truck. "Okay, so why are we here then?"

"You don't like surprises much, do you?" he asked as they met on the sidewalk.

"Not anymore."

"I'll keep that in mind moving forward. For now, though, just trust me on this, okay?"

At the door, she pointed at the hours listed on a placard. "It's after five, Seth. They're closed."

"True." Reaching into the pocket of his khaki pants, he retrieved a key and inserted it into the lock. "But Mom gave us permission, so we're good."

"Your mom has a key to town hall?"

"She does." He pushed the door open, motioned Penny to precede him inside, and then closed and locked the door behind them.

"Is she just supposed to let people use the key like this?" she asked.

"I'm not people, Penny. I'm her favorite son. Just don't tell my brother, okay?"

Her answering laugh echoed through the otherwise silent building. "Next question. *Why* is she letting you use it?"

"Look." Slowly, he made his way down the wide hallway, turning his head to the left and right with each step he took. When he reached the end, he turned, met her questioning eyes, and swept his hands toward the walls. "*Look.*"

"Look? Look at…" The rest of the question died on her lips as, following his lead, she looked to her left and spied a pair of familiar faces at what appeared to be a picnic of some kind. "Those are my grandparents!"

Spying a laminated card mounted to the right of the picture, Penny read the handwritten words aloud. "'Jonathan and Roberta Devons host a benefit picnic for the Collier family.'"

Again, she took in the couple she'd seen in countless pictures over the years—birthday pictures, holiday pictures, vacation pictures.

Penny stepped back, swung her gaze across the hall, and hurried over to another picture. In it, her grandfather appeared to be building a barn. Like the picnic photo, it too had a laminated card. "'Jonathan Devons works to help the Litner family rebuild their barn after a fire destroyed it,'" she read aloud.

She took a few more steps, passed another picture or two, and then stopped as the name on the neighboring card had her looking more closely at the costumed man depicted in the center. Sure enough, the eyes peering from the Santa Clause outfit belonged to her grandfather. On his lap were twin girls, each looking up at him with such awe it was hard not to smile.

"'Jonathan Devons brings Christmas to children in a local hospital,'" Seth read, stepping in beside Penny. "'For the fourth year in a row.'"

At a loss for what to say, she just stared at the picture. At the little girls' joy… At the man's strong knees holding them both upright… At the clearly homemade costume… At the white hair and the white beard… And, finally, at the kind eyes looking down at them…

"I don't know why he did what he did before he came to Deadwood, Penny. But it seems to me he changed his stripes once he did."

Penny abandoned her view of the man in the Santa suit for the one standing next to her, studying her, worrying about her. "You brought me here to see these?"

"I did."

"So, you knew these were here." It was a statement, not a question. But still, she waited for him to answer.

"I knew there were historical pictures here, sure." Seth led her down one side of the hall and up the other before settling himself against the wall closest to where she stood. "I've seen them dozens and dozens of times over the course of my life. But it wasn't until I talked to my mom this afternoon that she told me some of the pictures were of your grandfather. Then I knew I had to bring you here."

"None of this changes the fact that he stole from his own family," she said.

"I know it doesn't. But maybe it's an important footnote."

"Of?"

"A man who, for whatever reason—whether that was age, or your grandmother, or becoming a father, or something else—turned over a new leaf to become the person your mother told you about." Seth nudged her chin up with a gentle finger until he had her complete focus. "Someone who was kind and generous and selfless."

She heard Seth's words. Desperately wanted to believe them. But could she?

Slanting her gaze back to the picture, she tried to reconcile the man she found there with the one who stole from his parents and ran. A man who—

"Wait. Where'd his scar go?"

She looked at Seth, noted his furrowed brow and narrowed eyes, and then followed the path of his pointed finger to the man in the Santa suit.

"The scar above his right eyebrow," Seth continued as he leaned still closer to the picture. "It was in that shot you showed me from his book. But I don't see it here."

"I guess it healed."

"No. It was the kind of cut that'd been stitched closed. It was the kind that never goes away." Seth rubbed at his chin. "Scars on that area of the forehead? They don't ever go away. There's not enough excess skin to hide it."

"Yeah, but he had money, remember?" Penny countered. "Money he *stole*. He probably hired a cosmetic surgeon."

"In…" Seth consulted the laminated card. "December 1960? Nope, not buying it."

"I don't remember my grandfather having a scar in the picture on my parents' mantel." She looked from the picture to Seth as her thoughts traveled back to Tennessee and the picture that now resided on the shelf in her condo's living room. "Maybe you're confusing the picture I showed you the other day with something else you've seen recently? Maybe on your social media page or something?"

Seth was shaking his head before she'd even finished. "I don't do social media. Never have. And I know it was that picture because I asked if he had a sister, remember?"

Had he? She didn't—

"Wait! Yes! I remember now," said Penny, glancing at the small scar on Seth's forehead. "The doorknob incident, right?"

"Yep." He joined her in front of the framed photograph depicting the charity picnic and pointed at her grandfather. "No scar here, though, see? Or in the Santa one either."

Wordlessly, they both crossed to the picture of her grandfather in front of the barn. On the ground next to his feet was a toolbox not unlike Seth's. In one hand he held a hammer, in the other a nail, and above his eyebrow...no scar.

"Weird, right?" Seth mused.

"Very..." She froze, mid-nod, as Audrey Compton's shaky voice filled her head.

"Good-for-nothings is what they were."

She reached out, steadied herself on Seth's arm.

"Good riddance, I say. To both."

"Penny? What's wrong?"

Show her the man I know you to be, the one you've always been for anyone who cared to see beyond the matching exterior. "Oh my goodness. Seth!" Her steadying hand turned more grip-like as she stared up at Seth. "The inscription in my grandfather's book! And Audrey—she wasn't the one who was confused! I was."

"Audrey?" Seth repeated. "Who's Audrey?"

"My grandfather's stepsister, the one I spoke with yesterday. She pluralized things twice while talking about my grandfather." Penny let go of Seth's arm and hurried over to the Santa picture. "The caregiver warned me that Audrey was easily confused on account of dementia, and so I assumed that's what it was. But now..."

She drank in the pair of little girls and the way her grandfather met their collective awe with his own. She thought about the picture in her grandfather's book and how different it had felt compared to the one she'd looked at nearly every day of her life. She thought about the scar she'd never noticed before and the fact that it wasn't present in any of the pictures Seth had brought her to see. She thought about her great-grandmother's "matching exterior" comment. And then she knew. "My Grandpa Jon had a twin brother," she whispered.

Chapter Fourteen

She could feel Seth's nearness as she drew in a breath, pressed the top number on her phone's recent list and then the speaker button, and silently prayed that everything she'd come to believe over the past hour was, in fact, correct.

One ring…

Two rings…

"Compton residence, this is Milly."

"Milly, this is Penny McCormick. I called yesterday and spoke with Audrey," she said in a rush. "I was wondering if I could speak with her again? I have something else I need to ask her and—"

"No, I'm afraid Mrs. Compton will not be taking any more calls."

"But she has to!" At Seth's warning touch, Penny dialed down her tone. "Please, Milly. I won't keep her for more than a minute or two. I just need her to confirm something about—"

"Mrs. Compton took a turn for the worse last night and was taken to the hospital. They don't think she'll be coming home."

Penny sagged against Seth on his couch. "I-I'm sorry. I'm so, so sorry."

"Maybe *Milly* knows," Seth whispered.

She shook her head.

"If she's been with Audrey for a while, she might." Seth turned, his knees gently grazing Penny's. "Ask," he prodded. "There's no harm in that."

"Have you been with Mrs. Compton a long time, Milly?" she asked, meeting and holding Seth's eyes.

"Five years."

"I see." At Seth's nod of encouragement, she drew in another breath and released it with a hastily posed question. "Did Audrey ever mention someone by the name of Jonathan to you?"

Milly's laugh was quick, almost snort-like. "She did indeed. Referred to him as the stepbrother she never knew."

"The stepbrother she never knew?" Penny echoed.

"And the other one? I can't repeat what she called *him*."

Penny's eyes widened along with Seth's. "The *other* stepbrother?"

"That's right. Joe. They were twins."

She returned Seth's triumphant smile with one of her own while still keeping up with Milly. "Audrey didn't like Joe?"

Another laugh. "No, ma'am, she didn't. Why, I always knew when she'd gotten to that section in the paper on a clearheaded day. Because everything on the table would be rattling as she huffed and puffed. She'd toss the section on the table then pick it back up again. I used to tell her to stop looking if it bothered her so much, but you know how we women are about our mamas. We want to protect them even when they're not with us anymore."

Penny swallowed hard against the truth in Milly's words and, seconds later, the warmth of Seth's arm as it slid across her shoulders in a silent yet no less powerful show of understanding.

"That said, I hated seeing how worked up she'd get," said Milly. "Getting that upset always seemed to make the confusion worse in those early days."

"I don't understand. She got upset talking about Joe, or about something she read in the newspaper?" She slanted a glance at Seth to find him nodding along with her question.

"Both. But if Joe came up in conversation, it was because she brought him up. In the paper it was just about seeing the fruits she always felt should've been enjoyed by her mama...and by her, I imagine."

"Fruits?" Seth smacked a hand over his mouth then let it slide back down to accommodate the *sorry* he mouthed at Penny.

Seemingly unaware of the change in voice, Milly didn't miss a beat. "Joseph Homes is still the most popular builder in the greater Chicago area. Even today."

She didn't need to look at Seth to know he'd heard Milly's answer. The immediate cooling of her skin, where his arm had lingered far longer than a show of understanding normally dictated, told her that. "Are you saying that Joe started his own construction company in the wake of Devonshire Homes closing up shop?" Penny asked.

"From what Mrs. Compton said, Joe's company was *why* Devonshire Homes didn't make it. More resources, better marketing, and Joe was younger. But Mrs. Compton never understood why Joe couldn't have done the same thing with his daddy's company instead of going head-to-head and destroying it." Milly made a funny noise Penny couldn't fully decipher. She settled on disgust as the woman continued. "Can't say I don't wonder that myself, but not for me to judge, I suppose. That was for the Good Lord to decide twenty years ago when it was Joe's turn to stand before Him."

Twenty years ago.

Her great-uncle, Joe Devonshire, had still been alive when Penny was born.

It was a lot to take in, a lot to absorb. But she'd gotten what she needed from Milly, and for that, she was beyond grateful.

"You've answered my questions, Milly, thank you," Penny said. "I'll be—"

"May I ask as to your interest in all of this, Ms. McCormick?"

At Seth's shrug, she turned her gaze onto the leather-bound book she'd brought with her to Seth's house. "Jonathan Devonshire was my grandfather. And just as Audrey referred to him as the step-brother she never knew, Grandpa Jon died long before I was born." She considered leaving her explanation at that, but something inside her heart demanded she keep going. "With the recent death of my mom, I guess I just wanted to know things. Anything, really."

"There's a letter. With your grandfather's name on it."

Penny sat up tall. "A letter? From who?"

"I can't say. I just know I saw it one day when I was helping Mrs. Compton get her personal papers in order. It was inside one of her mama's files. I mentioned the old stamp and how the price of postage had gone up, but Mrs. Compton was so busy grousing about something, she didn't pay me or the letter any mind. And when I read your grandfather's name aloud, she got herself in such a tizzy I thought it best to just put the letter in the box along with everything else she was saving and let it be."

"Do you know if it's still there?" Penny asked. "In that same box?"

"I don't know why it wouldn't be. Once we put her papers in there, we never opened it again. But if you give me a few minutes, I'll check."

Penny's heart thumped hard inside her chest as she heard Milly put the phone down, walk across a clearly uncarpeted floor, open a door, let out a few grunts, close a door, walk back across the same floor and, finally, pick up the phone again.

"It's still here. Addressed to a Jonathan Devonshire at 15—"

"Sunrise Knoll. Deadwood, Oregon," Penny finished for Milly.

A beat of silence was soon followed by a more tentative Milly. "The return address says Richard Devonshire."

"My great-grandfather," Penny murmured.

More silence. A cough. More silence. And, finally, Seth's quiet voice in Penny's ear. "Ask her if she'll send it to you."

Could she? Should—

"I could mail it to you if you'd like," Milly offered.

"Oh Milly, that would be wonderful, if you think you could."

"Seems the only thing to do, seeing as how I just now found it in Mrs. Compton's things." Penny traded smiles with Seth as Milly continued. "I best be going if I'm going to make it to the post office before it closes for the day."

Penny pulled the book onto her lap and ran her fingers across the soft leather cover. "Thank you, Milly. You have no idea how much this means to me."

"As the last leaf on my own family's tree, I think I do, Ms. McCormick. I think I do."

"Did you manage to get some sleep?"

Penny stopped inside Seth's kitchen door and surveyed the various plates of deliciousness spread across the center of the table. "I think I did. Right up until my nose woke me up, anyway." She sniffed the air again and then motioned toward the food. "What is all of this?"

"Pot roast from my mom's recipe along with noodles and corn for sides."

"Oh Seth, you didn't need to go to all this trouble."

He filled a pitcher with ice water from the refrigerator door and carried it back to the table. "I like to cook. Always have. But I have to admit, it's way more fun when it's for someone other than just me."

"It…" She stepped closer, her stomach noisily reacting to the basket of homemade bread she spied just beyond the bowl of noodles. "It looks incredible."

"I'm glad." He pulled out the first of the two chairs and motioned her over. "Come. Sit."

When she was settled, he took the opposite chair and bowed his head in prayer. "Thank You, Lord, for Your many blessings. For good food, for needed answers, and for the kindness of strangers. Amen."

"Amen."

"Now, let's dig in." Seth handed her the serving platter of pot roast and waited as she took a slice and then sheepishly went back for another. "To this day, whenever I see Mrs. Koenig, my first-grade teacher, she always reminds me how, when asked what my favorite dinner was, I was the only kid who didn't say pizza or chicken nuggets. I said pot roast."

She took the gravy boat he offered, poured some on her meat, and breathed in the appetizing aroma. "I think this is the smell that woke me up."

"It is." He pointed his fork at his own plate. "It takes two hours to cook but starts smelling really good after the first thirty minutes. Which is why I used to drive my mom nuts asking when dinner would be ready on pot roast night. I'd ask, and I'd ask, and I'd ask."

She laughed. "I think I'd have asked a bunch too."

He waited while she tried her first bite, grinned as her eyes nearly rolled back in her head, laughed at the quiet moan that followed, and then dug into his own dinner. "I'll let Mom know you approve of her pot roast too."

"You sure you want to do that?" Penny teased. "Because that might encourage her even more."

A look she couldn't quite identify flitted across his face just before his shoulders rose and fell in a noncommittal shrug. Not sure what to make of the reaction, she opted for a bite of bread instead. "Oh. Wow. This is good too."

"Full confession. *That* is from a can."

"I won't tell a soul."

They continued eating, alternating between comfortable silence and animated conversation that covered everything from favorite songs and books to favorite pastimes. Finally, though, they were done, and Seth pulled his napkin off his lap and set it on the table with a satisfied smile. "Late but good."

She scanned the room until she found a clock. "It's ten o'clock!"

"It is."

Penny stood. "Oh Seth, I'm so sorry. I had no idea it was so late. You shouldn't have waited so long to eat."

"And if I hadn't, I'd have missed the nicest dinner I've had since the last one we shared together."

She reached for his empty plate and stacked it on top of her own. "You better be careful. A statement like that would be an easy ground ball for your mom."

The funny look was back. Only this time, instead of a non-committal shrug, there was a...*nod*? Before she could give it much thought though, the tingle of his hand against hers had her holding fast to the plates he tried to commandeer. "Oh no," she said, hurrying over to the sink. "You cook, I wash. No arguments."

"You wash, I dry," he countered. "No arguments."

Plate by plate and pot by pot, they made their way through clean-up duty with a modicum of efficiency considering she accidentally splashed him once, he not so accidentally splashed her back, and then she had to run around wiping up the areas of his kitchen that took the brunt of her retaliation.

When they were finally done, he directed her to the table and the laptop he'd set up while she'd been drying the floor. "What's this for?" she asked, pointing at the laptop.

"Didn't you want to look up Joseph Homes?"

She felt his shoulder brush against hers as he slid a chair into place next to her. "I do. Very much. But"—she looked again at the clock and then at Seth—"it's ten thirty now. I slept way longer than

I intended to when you suggested I get some rest. Don't you want to take me home now and maybe try this again tomorrow?"

"Nope. We've come this far. We need to finish it up."

For a moment, she simply studied him. The set of his determined jaw… The faint hint of stubble that ran along it… The fine lines next to his eyes when he was being earnest as he was, juxtaposed against the memory of their endearing crinkle during their unexpected water fight… The curve of his generous lips and her curiosity about how they'd feel if he kissed—

She didn't need a mirror to know the shock she'd surely see on her face over the thought of kissing Seth Foster. Then again, maybe she did, considering how quickly she felt it giving way to…*hope*?

The rapid tapping of his fingers broke through her woolgathering and, thankfully, mercifully, enticed her attention onto the computer screen in time to see him type *Joseph Homes Chicago* into the search bar. In little more than the blink of an eye, the first of several dozen pages of hits popped up, the first two of which was the Joseph Homes website and a decades-old news article about the death of Joseph Devonshire at the age of eighty-two.

Seth motioned for Penny to take control of the cursor and leaned toward the screen with her as she read her great-uncle's obituary.

Joseph Devonshire, founder and president of Chicago area's Joseph Homes, passed away in his sleep Monday afternoon after a short illness.

Devonshire splashed his way onto the homebuilding scene more than fifty years ago when he opened Joseph

Homes. With a keen eye for detail and an insatiable need to be the best, Devonshire captained Joseph Homes to the top, obliterating many of his competitors, including his father's company, Devonshire Homes—once known as the elite homebuilder in all of Chicago.

"Joe Devonshire was a force to be reckoned with in Chicago," said Tom Ruskin, a real estate attorney on the city's southside. "Which is why you'd be hard-pressed to come across anyone who's built a home in the last fifty years who didn't build with Joseph Homes."

Silently, Penny made her way down the rest of the obituary until she got to the final paragraph.

Devonshire was preceded in death by his father, Richard Devonshire, his mother, Vivian Devonshire, his brother, Jonathan Devonshire, his wife, Madeline, and his son-in-law, Christopher Reedy. He is survived by his daughter, Maureen Devonshire-Reedy, and his granddaughter, Samantha Reedy, both of Chicago.

"I have some cousins," Penny whispered. "Or at least I did twenty-three years ago."

Cousins.

She'd always wanted a cousin.

She looked at Seth's hand, allowed herself the comfort it brought, and then looked from him to the screen and back again. "I don't know what to do with this."

"You don't have to decide that right now, Penny. You've had a lot thrown at you in a short period of time. Let it digest. Read your great-grandfather's letter when it comes. And then see what feels right once you do."

This time when she studied him, she didn't care that he saw her doing it. Seth Foster was a nice guy, through and through. "I hope you know your mom has nothing to worry about," she said quietly.

CHAPTER FIFTEEN

In the nearly two weeks she'd been at the house, there were a handful of sounds Penny had come to relish.

The crackle and `snap of the wood each evening in the fireplace Seth had helped ready for use.

The thud of a paint can being closed as one more room was crossed off her to-do list.

The swish of sandpaper over a piece of furniture she was refinishing.

And the lighthearted strum of Seth's voice at her front door every morning, letting her know he was eager to start the next project.

Somehow, someway, Seth had managed to make the most mundane of tasks less cumbersome. When they painted, they played name-that-tune based purely on humming. When they cleaned, he fired up the playlist on his phone, and they sang along with song after song. When they tackled a particularly unappealing job, like removing the nests of critters who'd been living under the front porch for decades, he shared silly anecdotes about his family that had her listening more than thinking. And when they walked to the mailbox at the end of the driveway each day to see if her great-grandfather's letter had arrived, the quiet squeeze of his hand at the sight of the still-empty box helped lessen the sting.

Perhaps her favorite time, though, was in the early evening, when they called it a day on the task list and broke in her kitchen's new appliances by making some of their favorite childhood recipes for each other. Her mom's meatloaf… His mother's Brunswick stew… Her mom's chicken Parmesan… His mother's turkey tetrazzini. They moved around each other with ease as they traveled between the refrigerator and the stove, the cabinets and the oven. When it was her recipe, he set the table. When it was his recipe, she set the table.

The set of dishes had been her grandparents', and Penny loved that. She loved knowing that they, along with her mother as a young child and, later, as a teen, had sat at the same table, laughing and talking about their day just as she and Seth did. She still missed her mother nearly every second of every day, but the way in which she was missing her changed. Instead of feeling as if she were sitting in the middle of a giant hole all the time, she now found herself wishing she could tell her mom about the room they'd finished or her grandmother's pearl necklace they found wedged in the back of an empty dresser drawer or the way she felt when Seth was around.

"Penny for your thoughts, *Penny*?"

She looked up from the brush she was washing to find Seth studying her with a mixture of curiosity and amusement.

"See what I did there?" he joked.

Rolling her eyes, she shut off the water and rested the brush on the sink's edge, all signs of the sky-blue color she'd picked for her mother's childhood bedroom finally gone from its bristles. "So, so clever. Truly. You should consider a career in stand-up."

"Sarcasm doesn't become you."

Penny laughed. "Touché."

"The question still stands though."

"Question?"

Seth nodded. "What were you thinking about so hard just then?"

"I guess I was thinking about how close we are to being done."

He raked a hand through his paint-spattered hair, all signs of amusement gone. "Too close."

"Look, I know you're still upset about the notion of me renting this place out, but it's either that or sell it, and I'm not ready to do that."

Something sparked behind his eyes, and he stepped forward, closing the gap between them by a single footstep. "Not ready?"

"Mom was right. I feel them here." She tossed the paper towel into the trash and leaned back against the counter. "I'm not ready to give that up yet. I'm not sure I'll ever be. But that said, it seems silly to have it sit empty for what will likely amount to fifty-one weeks a year."

He recovered the step. Fast. "You see yourself only coming here one week a year?"

"Probably. Most likely in the summer when I can be outside. But we'll see how it—" She held up her finger at the distinctive *toot-toot* of a horn and then glanced at her watch. "Do you think that's the mail carrier?" she asked.

"Only one way to find out."

Penny took off at a run down the hall, out the door, across the front porch, and onto the driveway with Seth close on her heels. At the split, she went right around the giant oak tree and he went left. Penny reached the mailbox first. With a shaky hand, she opened the mailbox Seth had erected the morning after Milly's promise and squealed at the sight of the manila envelope with the Chicago address in the upper left-hand corner. "It's here," she whispered, staring into the box.

His only answer was the gentle squeeze of her hand.

She wasn't entirely sure how long she stood there, simply looking at the envelope, but however long it was, Seth never prodded, never pushed her to hurry. Eventually, she pulled it from the mailbox, opened it, and stared in at her grandfather's name in the center of the yellowed envelope it contained.

"It's really here," she said, pulling the envelope out and turning it over and over in her hands. "I've been waiting for this since Milly and I spoke, but now that it's here, I'm almost afraid to open it— afraid of what it might say."

"Faith is stronger than fear."

Penny's eyes snapped up to Seth's. "What did you say?"

"Faith is stronger than fear." Seth dug his hands into the front pockets of his blue jeans and shrugged. "It's something my mother always said to us kids when we were growing up. Still does sometimes."

She took a moment to breathe through the threat of tears sparked by his words and, when she was ready, she looked back at the letter. "Those were Mom's last words to me. Right after she told me she loved me."

Seth's hand found her shoulder and kneaded its way over to her neck as she flipped the envelope over and broke its nearly seventy-year-old seal with her finger. With hands that were shaking even more than before, Penny reached into the envelope, pulled out the letter, and slowly unfolded it.

With gathering emotion, she began to read aloud.

To my son, Jonathan,

It is not easy for a man to admit his mistakes. In order to do so, he must acknowledge that the consequences brought on by those mistakes are his alone to bear. For years, I refused to do that, confident that I knew best. But I did not. And for that, and so much more, I am truly sorry. I pray you will one day forgive me in a way I can never forgive myself.

Your mother, God rest her soul, tried to tell me I was creating a monster out of your brother by looking to you to clean up his messes. She was right. In asking you to do so, I didn't change his irresponsibility. I only emboldened it, teaching him to believe that his actions held no consequences and that disrespect was something that could always be swept under the carpet.

Time and time again, I looked to you to make things right. In doing so, I taught Joe to live life as he wished and I taught you to cover for him at all costs. What I got in return was one son who learned to care about no one but himself and another who felt he had to flee in order to finally live the life he should have been able to live all along.

That is my cross to bear.

At the time, all I saw was the company. My hopes for the company. My dreams for the company. I taught your brother to be dishonest, and he told me what I wanted to hear. You showed me what I wanted to see. For what it's worth, you are a talented craftsman. The proof of that can be found in all of the homes you worked on from the time you were a teen until you left. Maybe you would have continued if I'd only seen what I needed to see. But I didn't.

That is my cross to bear.

I taught your brother there were no consequences, and he stole the fiancée I all but forced you to love. And I proved him right again by looking the other way. It was easier for me to say boys will be boys and to see you running off as the actions of a sore loser.

But Madeline isn't why you ran. You ran because I taught you to believe Joe came before you did.

That is my cross to bear.

I know Joe slowly and methodically stole money from the company. I can't fault you for knowing it and not telling me. I wouldn't have believed you if you had, and you knew that. You'd gotten so adept at covering for him over the years that I'd come to see you as the black sheep, as I did in this case for far too long.

If it helps, my stupidity cost me the company. Joe used the money he stole from me to open his own company, Joseph Homes. I could have pressed charges, but the truth is he did what he did and became what he became because of me. I could have hung on a little longer, but what for? The end was near, so I beat it to the punch.

They were all painful lessons, Jonathan. The kind of lessons that would make any man bow his head in shame. But the greatest pain comes from realizing my actions—or lack thereof—cost me you and the opportunity to meet the woman who is finally deserving of your heart.

I pray that you will forgive me and that one day you will let me try to make amends. But if that day never comes, please know how very sorry I am.

Sincerely,

Your father

She looked up at Seth. "Grandpa Jon didn't do anything wrong. He ran because he didn't want to have to take the fall for his brother with something this serious—something that would've landed him in jail."

Seth's only answer came via a nod.

Again, she took in the letter, silently rereading it from start to finish. When she reached the end, she held it to her chest. "Why do you think Richard never sent this?"

"I can't answer that. Maybe he lost his nerve at the last minute? Maybe he asked Audrey's mom to mail it and she didn't?"

"Milly did say it was in Audrey's mother's things," she murmured, looking up from the letter once again. "But why wouldn't she have mailed it?"

"I don't know, Penny." It was a simple answer, but that didn't make it any less true.

They didn't know. Couldn't know.

"I wish Grandpa Jon could've known this."

"I do too. But that's why *you* have it now." Seth brushed a piece of hair off her forehead so gently she just barely felt his touch. But the warmth in his eyes? She felt that clear down to her toes. "So you can know it *for* him, Penny."

CHAPTER SIXTEEN

The mystery of her grandfather's words was solved.

The house was standing tall and ready for renters seeking a quiet getaway.

And the handful of bags she'd arrived in Deadwood, Oregon, with were packed in the trunk of her car in anticipation of her departure after breakfast with Seth's family the next morning.

She'd originally planned to hit the road before sunrise, but when she'd stopped by the hardware store to say goodbye to Rita, Rita had insisted Penny join them one last time. Reluctantly, she'd agreed, but now that it was less than twenty-four hours away, she was glad she had.

Seth and Rita and, by extension, their entire family, had become an anchor for her over the past few weeks. Instead of feeling alone as she had in Tennessee in the weeks following her mom's death, she felt as if she had people surrounding her who actually cared.

Regardless of the initial, underlying motive, Rita had known Penny would need someone to help with the house and sent Seth over to be that person.

Seth, who didn't agree with Penny's intention to rent the house, came by daily to help with its sprucing nonetheless.

Seth's sisters and brother and their families had not only made her feel welcome at the first family breakfast she'd crashed, they'd insisted she come back the next two Sundays as well.

Seth's nieces and nephew had showered her with drawings and half-eaten cookies at those gatherings just as they did Seth, following them up with whispered *I like you*'s.

Seth had made dinners fun again.

Seth had readily listened to dozens and dozens of stories about her mom and was always ready with a tissue when she was done.

Seth had shown her a side of her grandfather she'd never known at a time she most needed to see it.

And Seth had helped her find a truth she'd desperately needed.

"I'd offer a penny for your thoughts again, but I'm pretty sure I know what they are."

Startled, Penny toed her rocking chair to a stop and stared at the face looking back at her across the porch railing. "Seth! I didn't hear you drive up!"

"I'm not surprised." He hooked his thumb toward his truck and then made his way onto the porch to claim a spot on the top step. "Plotting your route home?"

A strange tightening in her throat had her rushing to clear her throat. "The car will tell me the way."

"Still coming to my house for breakfast before you shove off?"

"Are those blueberry muffins of yours still on the menu?"

"They are."

She cleared her throat a second time but to no avail. In fact, the tightening had morphed into the kind of lump that was usually a precursor to...*tears*? "Then I'll absolutely be there," she said while silently willing her eyes to remain dry. "And hoping you'll send me home with a few for the ride as well."

"I'll see what I can do."

"And maybe the recipe too?"

"Don't push it, Penny." He winked so she knew he was teasing and then continued. "Any last-minute things you want me to do around here before you go?"

"Nope. Everything is perfect, thanks to you."

He fidgeted his hands along the edge of the step on which he sat and then stood, a growing restlessness fairly oozing from his pores. "I imagine your renters will be pleased."

"I imagine they will be."

He wandered down the steps only to turn and make his way back up to her rocker's lone mate. Dropping onto it, he rocked for a few seconds, stopped, and then rocked again, his feet undecided as to the pace he should set.

"Are you okay?" she finally asked when she could no longer ignore the countless signs that he wasn't.

Seth stopped, looked up at the porch ceiling, and blew out a long, steady breath. "I'm trying to respect what you're doing here, Penny, I really am. But it's hard."

She waited for him to give up on the ceiling. When he finally did, she was waiting. "I'm willing to take it slowly. See how it goes."

He stopped rocking. "You are?"

"For a little while, anyway. "

The smile she'd come to adore began in the left corner of his mouth and quickly spread to the right. "Penny, you have no idea how—"

"Yes, I do. You've told me, numerous times, remember?"

His smile dulled. "I've told you what numerous times?"

"That you don't want 'a parade of strangers' in Deadwood. And I want to respect that. I want to give you and everyone else in town a chance to get used to it, to see the benefits it can bring if you're open to it." She toed her own rocker to a stop but remained seated as she looked out over the trees lining the front end of the property—some of which her grandfather may very well have planted. "So, to that end, I'm thinking I'll just put it on the vacation rental site for summer months at this time. That way there aren't strangers driving around while the kids are coming and going from school."

"Summer months," Seth repeated.

"Yes." She closed her eyes and breathed in the aroma of chimney smoke somewhere in the distance. "Does that work better? At least for now?"

When he didn't answer, she parted her lashes to find him staring out at the same trees she'd been looking at moments earlier. Only it was clear, by the glassiness of his eyes, that he wasn't seeing them. "Seth?"

He opened his mouth to speak, closed it, and then rested his head against the back of the rocker. "What did you decide about your family in Chicago? Are you going to reach out to them?"

It was an odd shift in conversation, but since he posed it, she went with it. "I've considered it. A lot, actually. But I think I've decided I'm going to let it go."

"Why?" He stopped rocking and turned the chair to face Penny. "I thought you were excited about the idea of having blood relations, especially a cousin."

"I was," she admitted. "But this Maureen? Her mother was Madeline Devonshire."

"Okay…"

"Madeline was the one my grandpa Jon was engaged to marry. The one who dumped him for Joe."

"Okay…"

She stared at Seth, willing him to understand. "You saw the letter, Seth. That breakup is one of the reasons my grandfather ran. She *hurt* him."

"True. But doesn't that mean Madeline is also the reason he found your grandmother?"

It was an answer she hadn't expected and one she couldn't deny. "I hadn't really thought of it that way," she whispered as her mind's eye played out the rest of that truth—a truth that led to the birth of her own mother and, eventually, Penny, herself. "But she still hurt him. Why would I want to have anything to do with Madeline and Joe's daughter or granddaughter?"

Seth scooted forward on his chair until their knees touched. "Do you remember what I said when you said your grandfather had done something awful?"

She considered his question for a moment, her thoughts wondering in and out of the countless conversations they'd had on the subject, until, finally, she hit on the one she knew he was referencing. "You said that nothing about what my grandfather may or may not have done changed who my mom was or who I am."

"I stand by those words," Seth said. "For you and your mom, and for your cousins. What Joe did is on Joe. What Madeline did is on Madeline. Their daughter and granddaughter shouldn't pay the price for that. If you meet them and they're awful too, then that's a different story. But until they show that, I think they—and you—deserve the benefit of the doubt."

"But—"

He quieted her protest with the tip of his finger. "Worst case, you're exactly where you are now. Best case, you have family. I don't see how you lose, either way."

She captured his hand inside hers and held it to her cheek. "Seth Foster? One day, when the time is right for you, you're going to make some woman a very, *very* lucky gal."

CHAPTER SEVENTEEN

One by one, Seth's family members stopped en route to their cars to say goodbye to Penny. His sister, Lisa, her husband, Brad, and their daughters, Kayla and Minnie... His other sister, Dana, Dana's husband, Marty, and their son, Carter... His brother, Doug, and Doug's wife, Lila... And Seth's dad, Tom... Each set of arms that enveloped her, each *we'll miss you* spoken was accompanied with such genuine affection and earnestness it stirred up something Penny hadn't felt since her mother's passing.

Somehow, despite her only being in Deadwood for just a few weeks, she felt as if she'd been there her whole life. From the outside looking in, she knew it made no sense. But inside? Where the ache over leaving these people was making it so she could barely speak lest she break into tears? It was as real as real could be.

"Well, sweetheart, I don't know what to say." Rita gathered Penny's hands inside her own and held them tight. "Encouraging you to come here, even for just a little while, was the most beautiful gift your mama could've possibly given me and my family."

Penny squeezed back. "Thank you for being someone I could talk to about her and about my grandparents. You helped make them feel less far away."

"They're right here"—Rita touched the tip of her finger to Penny's head and then dropped it down to her heart—"and right here. Always. All of those wonderful moments you had with her are yours to revisit anytime you want in your memories. I know I visit with her in mine all the time. Sometimes those memories make me laugh, and sometimes they bring tears to my eyes. But how blessed I am to have them."

Overcome with emotion, Penny swept her gaze to the departing cars and the hands that waved from their windows and then to Seth, waiting patiently on the porch for his turn to say goodbye, the sadness she saw in his face only intensifying her own.

"When I met you that first day at the shop, you said your mama wanted you to come to your grandparents' house so you could feel them, yes?" At the single nod of confirmation Penny was able to manage, Rita hooked her thumb beneath Penny's chin and nudged upward until their gazes met. "Did you?"

"More and more with each passing day," Penny said. "Only…"

She stopped. Swallowed. Skittered her focus back to Seth.

"Only *what*, Penny?" Rita prodded.

"Only it wasn't the house that made me feel her most. It was you. It was your family. And…" She felt her heart rate accelerate as Seth shoved his hands into his pockets and stepped off his front porch, heading toward them.

The faintest hint of a smile niggled at the corner of Rita's mouth. "And?"

She took in the subtle wave of his sun-bleached hair, the way the sun seemed to find and accentuate the amber flecks in his eyes, the determined set of his strong jaw, and the quiet humility he wore like a comfortable old shirt, and let it all fade to the background of what she loved most about Seth Foster.

The way he listened.

The way he supported her in his words and in his actions.

The way he made her smile.

The way he held her when she cried.

And the way he always seemed to know the right words at the right times…

"And your son," Penny whispered.

"Seth never knew your mama."

"I know. But nine weeks ago, when I lost her, I was determined never to love anyone with my whole heart ever again because the pain of losing someone I loved that much was simply too awful."

"And now?"

"And now I realize that walking away from that kind of love is every bit as painful."

Seth stepped into the space occupied by his mother just moments earlier and gently cupped Penny's face with his hands. "So *don't* walk away, Penny. Stay. Work from here. Cover your fridge with pictures from my nieces and nephew. And let me finally have the woman I've been holding my mom off for all this time."

A flurry of movement just over Seth's shoulder captured her attention just long enough to giggle at Rita's prayer-clasped hands before returning her undivided, albeit tear-filled attention to the handsome man wearing his heart on his sleeve as he waited for the only answer she could give.

"I'll stay."

Chapter Eighteen

Eighteen Months Later

"Knock, knock, may I come in?"

Penny looked at the elegantly dressed woman peeking around her bedroom door and smiled from deep inside her soul. "Rita, of course. Come in. I could use a little help getting this wreath secured good enough that it won't fall off the second I walk down my porch steps."

"Oh Penny, you look absolutely beautiful," Rita gushed as she pushed the door closed in her wake and then hurried over to the mirror-topped vanity. "My son is one very lucky young man."

"Trust me, Rita, I'm the lucky one in this equation."

She released her hold on the wreath's built-in comb and watched as Seth's mother stepped in and worked her magic, gently securing the flowered headpiece in place while Penny added a hint of gloss to her lips and a touch of mascara to her eyelashes. "The side yard looks positively breathtaking, sweetheart. You and Seth did a marvelous job."

"Thank you. We wanted it to be perfect for today."

"And you succeeded."

"Is everyone here?" Penny asked as she capped up her gloss and placed it inside the drawer.

Rita finished arranging Penny's soft curls across her shoulders and stepped back, nodding. "If by everyone you mean the entire town of Deadwood, then yes, they're all here."

"And Maureen? Samantha?"

"They are sitting in the front row right next to Tom and me."

"Perfect." Penny studied her reflection for a long moment and then lifted her gaze to Rita's. "This is the happiest day of my life, and Mom isn't here to see it."

Lowering herself to the edge of Penny's bed, Rita set her clutch atop her lap and snapped it open. "Your mama might not be here physically, but she's here, Penny. She's here in this house she brought you to, she's in that pearl necklace of hers you're wearing, she's in that beautiful smile you bless my son with every single day, and she's in *this*."

Penny turned her back on her own curious expression to get a closer look at the yellowed square of paper in her soon-to-be mother-in-law's hand. "What is it?"

"I found it in my hope chest last night while I was looking for something else." Rita handed it to Penny. "Open it."

Slowly, Penny unfolded the paper to its original size and stared down at the childlike writing that covered it from one side to the other.

Penny,
I love you!!
Forever and always!!!
Love,
Your mommy

"What *is* it?" Penny repeated so softly she could barely hear herself.

"That's your mom letting you know she loves you via her eight-year-old self."

She took in the pencil smudges... The big letters... The exclamation points... And— "I promised myself I wouldn't cry today," she said on the heels of a long, steadying breath.

"Then don't."

Pulling the letter to her chest, Penny encircled Rita in a hug. "Thank you for this. It's...it's perfect."

"I'm glad, sweetheart. Now, *please*, go marry my son."

Dear Readers,

When I take stock of my many blessings in life, my friendship with Emily Quinn is one of the dearest. We met in 2006 when she won a contest I ran on a multi-author blog. When I saw her mailing address for receiving the prize, I realized she lived in the same general area I did. So I took a chance and offered to meet her in person. That single act of courage (or insanity if you think about stranger danger) has resulted in the kind of friendship that has forever imprinted itself on my heart.

Fast forward to now. Despite my moving halfway across the country just three years after that first meeting, our friendship is stronger than ever. We email each other daily, talk on the phone often, and travel together for book (and fun!) reasons whenever possible

Needless to say, when the opportunity came up to write this book together, it was an immediate *yes, please*! Our writing careers have always had us in the same arena, but this was a chance to brainstorm a project together, having parts of her story lead to mine, and making it all fit together.

Emily and I sincerely hope you enjoy your time in Deadwood, Oregon, with Jonathan and Roberta (from Emily's story), and Penny and Seth (from my story).

Wishing you the blessings of friendship,

Laura & Emily

About the Authors

Emily Quinn

Emily Quinn loves hanging out in her Tennessee home watching for deer and cooking new recipes when she's not thinking of stories to keep her busy on the keyboard. She shares her cabin in the woods with her husband and two Keeshonds who think they rule the house, if not the world.

Laura Bradford

While spending a rainy afternoon at a friend's house as a child, Laura Bradford fell in love with writing over a stack of blank paper, a box of crayons, and a freshly sharpened number-two pencil. From that moment forward, she never wanted to do or be anything else.

When she's not writing, Laura loves to bake, travel, and advocate for those living with MS.

Story Behind the Name

Deadwood, Oregon

Deadwood is located on Oregon Route 36, in the forested area of the state. The town was named after Deadwood Creek that runs nearby. The creek was named from the timber snags that built up next to the banks. Jonathan, in the first novella, is working at a lumber mill that used Deadwood Creek to move the logs from the forest where the trees were cut. Today, Deadwood's population is decreasing, but local artists have renovated the old schoolhouse for their residence, hoping to revitalize the town.

Seth Foster's Blueberry Muffins

Ingredients:

½ cup butter or margarine, softened

1 cup sugar

2 eggs

2 cups all-purpose flour

2 teaspoons baking powder

½ teaspoon salt

½ cup milk

1 teaspoon vanilla extract

2½ cups fresh blueberries

Sugar to sprinkle on top

Directions:

Preheat oven to 375 degrees.

Grease (or use liners) 12-cup muffin pan.

In large bowl, cream butter and sugar until light and fluffy. Add eggs one at a time, beating well after each addition.

In a separate bowl, combine flour, baking powder, and salt. Add alternately to creamed mixture with milk and vanilla.

Fold berries into batter and spoon into muffin pan. Sprinkle with sugar. Bake for 15 to 20 minutes until golden brown.

*Read on for a sneak peek of another exciting book
in the Love's a Mystery series!*

Love's a Mystery *in*
Gnaw Bone, Indiana
by Johnnie Alexander & Dana Lynn

The Thistle Rings
By Johnnie Alexander

Scotland

April 1934

The old man stirred in his sleep, muttering the words Kenna Calhoun had heard him say whenever the dark days of his past especially troubled his soul. *Cor nobile, cor immobile.* A noble heart is an immovable heart.

"I'm here, *Seanair*," Kenna said, using the Gaelic term for grandfather. She rested the back of her hand on his forehead and breathed a sigh of relief that although his pale skin warmed her fingers, the burning heat was gone. At least for now.

"My lovely Kenna," he murmured, his eyes half-opening, his mind confused. "*Mo chridhe.*" My heart.

The endearment meant his thoughts weren't on Kenna but on *Seanmhair*, the grandmother who'd died a few days before Kenna's birth. In those dreaded dark days, the grieving widower found comfort only in the sweet innocence of his precious granddaughter. As if she'd been born to restore his joy and his purpose.

"I'm here," Kenna murmured, not caring if he believed her to be the wife he'd adored. He loved Kenna too. At this moment, only that mattered. "Are you thirsty?"

Without waiting for an answer, she poured a glass of water from the pewter pitcher on the washstand and held the glass to his lips. He managed only a sip or two before drifting again into sleep while mouthing the Latin words.

Cor nobile, cor immobile.

The once great Granvilles, who had amassed lands and power long, long ago and had been given their title during the reign of Queen Anne, had taken the Latin phrase as their motto. From their beginning, the mighty Granvilles never failed to have a Calhoun by their side. At first as trusted warriors and bodyguards, later as stewards of their great estate.

Until those dark days, when a boating accident took the lives of the sixth duke, the duke's heir, and Seanair's chridhe. Steward Calhoun almost died himself in his attempts to save his wife, his best friend, and the young man born to take his father's place.

Kenna returned to the old wooden rocker made more comfortable by cushions she'd stitched herself. Her rocking soon adjusted to the rhythmic rise and fall of Seanair's chest. A few more months, the doctor had said. Beyond that…

She dozed, falling into a dreamless sleep, then jerked awake to her grandfather's shout.

"I must find him," he bellowed as he fought a losing battle with the blankets. "Where is he? Where did she take him?"

Kenna rushed to his side. "Shh, Seanair. You must sleep."

"He's lost." Tears swam in her grandfather's pale blue eyes, and his arthritic fingers dug into her skin with more strength than she expected him to have. "His grandson is lost."

"Not lost, Seanair. He's safe. You've always told me his mother took him away to protect him."

Her grandfather shook his head, and spittle ran down his chin. "He must claim what is his. It's only right. We must find him."

Kenna cleaned his chin with a soft cloth, her mind overflowing with Seanair's wondrous stories of his years on the estate, first as the companion to the future sixth duke then as his steward when the title became his.

The glory days of grand balls, rousing hunting parties, and bountiful harvests, Seanair always insisted, would never return. Not because the world changed after being caught in a horrific war, but because a pretender claimed the title that did not belong to him.

Kenna smoothed the blankets, and her grandfather drifted into a restless sleep. His long fingers twitched, as if grasping at something only he could see. She longed to find the words to put his mind at ease. Instead, Seanair would go to his grave carrying the weight of a burden he couldn't put down.

She kissed Seanair's soft cheek then wandered to the leaded pane window. Dawn was still hours away, and the moon's sliver hid behind heavy clouds. For as long as she could remember, the story of the lost Granville heir had played in her imagination.

On warm summer days, Kenna would climb high into her favorite tree, a graceful rowan whose berries were gathered each autumn and made into jam. Perched on her favorite limb, her back resting against the trunk, she imagined fantastical stories where she traveled to distant lands seeking the sixth duke's lost grandson.

In her childish stories, she found him in brutal poverty, working his fingers to the bone for a master as despicable as any who inhabited Charles Dickens's thrilling novels. As heroine of her own tale, Kenna whisked the boy away from the cruelty and restored him to his true home.

As she got older, romance entered her stories. She revealed to the missing heir his true identity, and he asked for her hand in marriage. Together they returned to Granville Hall to live happily ever after. During those years, Kenna was never quite sure if she was more in love with the mysterious heir or the prospects of living on the grand estate.

She smiled now, remembering those silly imaginings. Though, in the quiet of the pre-dawn hours and affected by her grandfather's pleas, she dreamed again of being the heroine of the story. The one who found the sixth duke's grandson, the true and legal seventh duke. The one who took away Seanair's burden.

If only… Her gaze shifted to the narrow desk pushed into a corner of the spacious room. Until a few years ago, Seanair occasionally received letters all the way from America, which he read in private and hid away. He'd answer no questions about them but was withdrawn and moody for days after receiving one.

Were the letters in that desk? Could they give her the clue she needed to fulfill her quest?

Gnaw Bone, Indiana
Two Weeks Later

Only a few coins clinked in Liam McIver's pocket as he followed the path across tree-thick hills from the artist's colony to the post office in Gnaw Bone.

Liam knew from painful experience during his stays in prior years that the colony manager never allowed unpaid extensions. Penniless artists with more hopes than cents had burned him once too often. "Unkept promises don't put food on the table or fresh linens on the bed," the man was fond of saying.

If the commission check wasn't in today's post, Liam would have to beg Miss Alice, the cheerless landlady at the town's board-inghouse, to take mercy on him. Maybe he could offer to do chores around the place to earn his room and board. He wouldn't mind the manual labor. Maybe he needed hard work to shake him from this dry spell.

It was the nature of art. Multiple commissions then nothing. His latest sculpture, an Indianapolis sportsman's favorite retriever, was received with such admiration that Liam had counted on his client to recommend him to friends, neighbors, and business associates.

With his expectations high, Liam whiled away too many hours at the Liars Bench on the town square, either listening to the old-timers' tall tales and gossip or playing an occasional game of horseshoes. But over three weeks had gone by and the promised references, like the promised check, had yet to arrive.

Turned out the frugal manager was right about unkept promises.

Now, needing money and unable to appeal to his parents, Liam was drained of creativity and desperate for that mysterious spark to speak to him. The desperation led to fear.

What if the spark never touched him again?

Liam couldn't bear for his artistic dreams to die, but his more immediate concern was his lodging fee. At the Whippoorwill Glen Artist Colony—a sprawling house with rooms to let to working artists, well-tended gardens, and a rustic simplicity beyond the manicured lawns—Liam had learned to trust his artistic sensibilities and gained experience. He'd been coming to the colony for a few weeks each spring since he was eighteen.

Five years. And yet, if he didn't pay his bill, he'd be out the door.

Liam fingered the gold ring he wore on a chain around his neck and briefly wondered what the proprietor of the Gnaw Bone pawn shop would give him for the old thing with its strange Latin inscription.

Better to go hungry and sleep under Miss Alice's front porch, though, than risk Mother's wrath if he couldn't redeem it. The ring meant something to her—a secret she promised to tell him someday. He doubted it was anything worth knowing. Mother loved mystery novels, especially ones written by that English woman, Agatha Christie. Liam supposed his mother needed a mystery of her own to add excitement to her routine life.

If the check didn't come, Liam could pawn something else. His art supplies. His sculpting tools. The clothes off his back. He shook his head, knowing he couldn't do it. The ridiculous ring would go before he gave up the tools of his trade or dug secondhand clothes out of the missionary barrel.

He breathed a prayer as he opened the post office door that today would be the day his trust in the sportsman was reborn. He hoped the Almighty paid attention to informal prayers said outside of church and when Liam wasn't on his knees. It seemed Jesus had also done a lot of His praying outdoors. Liam should talk to the reverend about that sometime.

"Good morning, Mr. McIver." The postmaster pulled an envelope from a slot in the shelves behind him. "If you'd allow us to deliver your mail to Whippoorwill Glen, you wouldn't need to come to town to retrieve it."

"I enjoy the walk." Besides, Liam would crawl through the woods rather than risk his mail getting lost after it left the post office. Or even worse, stolen.

The postmaster's dour expression didn't change, and his tone dripped with condescension. "Here you are then, sir." He handed over the envelope then stepped away from the counter.

Relief swooshed through Liam when he read the return address, but he refrained from ripping open the envelope. His mother expected him to behave like an Old World gentleman even though he wasn't one. "One doesn't need a silver spoon in one's mouth to eat like one does," was one of her frequent aphorisms.

Liam didn't think the saying made sense nor did he know why she ignored the typical "born with a silver spoon" phrase. But Mother wouldn't be Mother if she didn't put on airs as if she were royalty.

He thanked the postmaster then stepped outside. Unable to wait a moment longer, he leaned against the outer wall, slit open the envelope, and stared at the unexpected dollar amount on the check. The accompanying note from the sportsman apologized for the delay and confirmed the amount was intended as a bonus.

Liam uttered a prayer of thanks as he tucked the envelope into his pocket. Next stop the bank then the general store. Maybe he'd even treat himself to a meal at the hotel restaurant. The cook at Whippoorwill Glen fed the guests well, but the menu at the hotel would be a nice change.

As Liam pushed away from the wall, Old Jim, a local jack-of-all trades, passed by on a farm wagon pulled by his swayback mare. A young woman of about Liam's age perched on the seat beside Old Jim. Red curls fell beneath a dark blue bonnet that framed a pale face. Her head turned as her gaze darted from one side of the street to the other then landed on him. She stared, her mouth set in a determined line.

If they'd met before, he would have remembered such a beauty. But just in case, he smiled and bowed his head. She stared a moment longer then turned to Old Jim. It was impossible to hear what she said, but Old Jim responded with a shake of his head. She grabbed his arm, seemingly insistent, and he pulled back on the reins. The team had barely stopped before the woman climbed down from the wagon without waiting for Jim to assist her. The old man glared at her as if she had two heads.

Liam headed toward her, but then a horse's neighing caught his attention. The rider of a glossy black thoroughbred with a flowing mane circled in the wide street behind the wagon instead of passing on the other side. He too glared at the girl.

Liam picked up his pace, reaching her as she slid past the wheel and twisted to face him with a huge smile.

"I wasn't sure you'd be here to meet me." Her accented voice quavered, but her gaze and smile held steady. "How nice of you to do so. Perhaps you will be so kind as to escort me to my lodgings, and we can talk along the way." She tucked her gloved hand in the crook of his arm.

"I'm sorry, miss," Liam began, "but I don't know—"

"Is there a hotel nearby? Or perhaps a boardinghouse?" She darted a glance to the rider on the black horse. The smile faded, and the grip of her hand tightened on his arm.

She turned back to him and lowered her voice. "Please, I am in need of an escort. Will you help me?"

Liam gazed into those large eyes and knew he could refuse her nothing. "Of course I'm here," he said loudly. "I've been counting the hours until your arrival."

Her smile, as bright as a ray of sunshine on a rainy day, returned. "You are too kind. Would you mind carrying my bag?"

"Why else am I here?" Liam said lightly. As he took the carpet-bag from Old Jim, he avoided eye contact with the rider on the black gelding. But the hair standing up on the back of his neck and the tingling down his spine told him the rider now glared at him.

Liam hoped the lass with the red curls could tell him why.

A NOTE FROM THE EDITORS

We hope you enjoyed another volume in the Love's a Mystery series, created by Guideposts. For over seventy-five years, Guideposts, a nonprofit organization, has been driven by a vision of a world filled with hope. We aspire to be the voice of a trusted friend, a friend who makes you feel more hopeful and connected.

By making a purchase from Guideposts, you join our community in touching millions of lives, inspiring them to believe that all things are possible through faith, hope, and prayer. Your continued support allows us to provide uplifting resources to those in need. Whether through our communities, websites, apps, or publications, we inspire our audiences, bring them together, and comfort, uplift, entertain, and guide them. Visit us at guideposts.org to learn more.

We would love to hear from you. Write us at Guideposts, P.O. Box 5815, Harlan, Iowa 51593 or call us at (800) 932-2145. Did you love *Love's a Mystery in Deadwood, Oregon*? Leave a review for this product on guideposts.org/shop. Your feedback helps others in our community find relevant products.

Find inspiration, find faith, find Guideposts.

Shop our best sellers and favorites at
guideposts.org/shop

Or scan the QR code to go directly to our Shop

Printed in the United States
by Baker & Taylor Publisher Services